THE
STEADFAST
HEART
By Arlem Hawks

Titles by Arlem Hawks

The Steadfast Heart

Other Titles in the Forever After Series:

Beauty and the Baron, by Joanna Barker
The Captain and Miss Winter, by Sally Britton
The Steadfast Heart, by Arlem Hawks

THE
Steadfast
HEART

FOREVER AFTER

ARLEM HAWKS

To two of the best people I have ever known—

Mary Carol, who has shown me how to smile
through the hard times,

and Grandpa Bob, who taught me no one is too
lost to love.

"Prettiest of all was a little lady who stood at the castle's open door. She too was cut out of paper, but she wore a frock of the clearest gauze and a narrow blue ribbon over her shoulders, like a scarf . . .

"'That would be just the wife for me,' thought he, 'if she were not too grand. But she lives in a castle, while I have only a box, and there are five and twenty of us in that. It would be no place for a lady. Still, I must try to make her acquaintance."'

From "The Steadfast Tin Soldier,"
by Hans Christian Andersen

Chapter One

Robert Brenton didn't know the point of coming to a ball if he couldn't dance. Blast it, he couldn't even walk across the floor for a drink without his foot announcing to the world he was on the move. *Here comes the broken man!* it shouted with every clap against the dance floor's planks. *And there he goes!*

He glowered at the offending limb, which ended half way down his calf. Light from chandeliers above glinted across the cherry wood, smoothed into a semblance of a foot. He had a boot specially made to cover the foot, but one didn't wear boots to balls. Not in Bath, at least. He hadn't bothered with commissioning dance shoes to fit. Still, the wooden foot looked better than the peg leg he had worn the last two years.

If he had taken one step back when he heard the blast . . .

"Brenton, there you are."

Robert pushed himself up from his seat, trying to rise with an air of ease. Lanky Spencer Addison

1

gripped his shoulder, a grin splitting his face. "I didn't think we would see you here tonight."

"You secured me an invitation and insisted I attend. How could I have refused?" In truth, he'd come to Bath hoping to escape the constant social obligations of his father and brother, but one couldn't visit Bath without attending at least one ball.

Addison lowered his voice. "You've refused all the other invitations since returning to England." There was no accusation in his tone, only concern that made Robert want to return to hiding in his corner. No one saw his face anymore. Only the foot.

"It's been nearly two years. It's time." Robert laughed, hoping to dispel the gloom. The laugh didn't come so easily as it once had. "What friends have you made in my absence? Surely you have introductions to make."

"I am certain I can find several, if you feel inclined to meet people."

A violin called out the start of the next set, and the strains of music helped mask Robert's progression to the other side of the room with his companion. He watched the dancers, begrudging them their smiles and laughs. Once he could dance and flirt as well as any gentleman.

No more.

At the top of the set, a striking young woman wove through the line. She threw her coquettish smile at every young man who ventured a glance, which wasn't difficult as she stood half a head taller than the other ladies in the line, blonde locks

2

gleaming in the candlelight. Her foam-white gown, touched with blue ribbon, swished about as she maneuvered an expert turn.

Robert chuckled. Now there was a girl who knew she had the eyes of all the room and meant to enjoy it.

A lady stopped his friend as they passed. "Mr. Addison, how good it is to see you."

Robert continued to watch the graceful dancer as Addison conversed. She never tired, despite the demands of the dance. Her companions' leaps had already lost their lightness, but she continued to spring with limitless energy, her bright curls giving a pleasing bounce with each movement.

Two years ago, he would have been first in line to engage her for the next set. Now he could only admire her from afar.

"Forgive me, this is Lieutenant Brenton, an old friend of mine from the navy." Addison's hand on his arm drew Robert back into the conversation.

"Ah, yes," the lady said. "I believe I have met your brother, the one to inherit Aston Park in Wiltshire."

"Gerald, yes. My eldest brother."

"I hear he is to be married. I congratulate your family."

Robert laughed to clear the twinge of jealousy. Good old Gerald always had all the luck. First born, a favorite with the ladies, and now a pretty bride with a sizable dowry.

"Why are two fine young gentlemen such as yourselves not dancing?" the woman asked.

His and Addison's eyes dropped to Robert's wooden foot. The lady's face paled.

"I am deeply sorry, sir. I did not see it!"

Robert almost snorted. In the breeches demanded by polite society, it was hard not to notice the dark piece of wood where a stocking and shoe should have been.

"Did you lose it in the war?" she asked.

Most would have found offense in her impertinent question, but Robert didn't mind. "Trafalgar, madam." She gave him the usual wide-eyed awe that particular battle's name drew in conversation.

It was Robert's sign to exit, lest he draw her pity. With a bow, he excused himself to sit. The stump at the end of his right leg throbbed with each step as he returned to his seat. He lowered himself into the chair with the help of his arms, then sat back to watch the fair-haired dancer prance about the room. His fingers came up to scratch under his jaw, the odd action he found soothed some of the phantom itching from his missing foot.

Every moment served as a reminder of what he no longer had, and the normal life he could no longer aspire to.

Miles Pelham was darkly handsome, irresistibly charming, fabulously wealthy, and he belonged completely to Holly Addison.

She took great pleasure in the envious and longing stares they received as she put her hand in his to promenade down the set. Best to enjoy their dancing days while they could, as after the wedding it wouldn't be acceptable to dance together. Though she hated to deprive Society of such a spectacle, she could hardly stand waiting the one hundred and fifty-three days until she became Mrs. Miles Pelham. If only Mama hadn't set her heart on getting the marriage clothes in London.

Holly held her head high at the perfect angle for spectators to admire her profile and catch her adoring gaze into Mr. Pelham's eyes. She couldn't think of two people better suited to marry, for they were both young, attractive, and rich.

Four years ago, Mr. Pelham wouldn't have spared a second glance in her direction.

Holly faltered in her step, but hid it with a little skip that turned the movement into added style rather than a mistake. Her past liked to reaffirm its presence in her thoughts more often than she liked. But soon none of that would matter. She would leave the Addison name and any lingering gossip behind.

At the end of the dance, she curtsied and gave Mr. Pelham the smile he particularly liked with lowered lashes. He'd been more reserved than usual tonight, no doubt owing to the late hour he'd stayed at the gentlemen's club the night before, but he'd perked up as they danced. Just as he always did. She wrapped her gloved hand around the arm of his well-tailored suit, and he led her back to her parents. Her mother beamed at the sight of them walking together.

She stood, reaching out to fuss over one of Holly's sleeves that didn't need fixing. Holly batted her hand away. She wasn't the seventeen-year-old child anymore who had little knowledge of how to properly dress. But Mama didn't see that, never mind that Holly had just passed her twenty-first birthday. Mama only saw the gentleman and his 4,000 pounds, and wanted to keep her daughter looking the part of his intended bride. Holly didn't know if she or her mother was more pleased with Mr. Pelham.

"How have you enjoyed the dance, sir?" Mama crooned as Holly's betrothed bowed over her hand in greeting. "The whole room is abuzz over the two of you."

Mr. Pelham slipped Holly a sly glance. "Have they liked the view?"

Mama beat her fan and leaned in excitedly. "We liked it immensely."

"Then I think we should give them another show. Will you save me the next dance, my darling Miss Addison?"

Holly beamed. She would. And the next dance after that, and the next. They couldn't disappoint their audience, of course.

"Will you excuse us a moment, Mr. Pelham?" Her mother caught her hand and drew her away.

"Your brother wished to see you," she said in a hushed tone. "He wanted to introduce you to one of his friends from the navy, despite my protests." The woman's eyebrows shot up and her lips pulled tightly together.

Mama hated the very mention of the navy. That they had been forced to send their only son off, possibly to his death, at such a young age never sat well with her, even seventeen years later. She did her best not to associate with any of Spencer's comrades, which always sent a pang through Holly's heart.

Not that she usually enjoyed the company of the officers Spencer brought home. They talked of nothing else but navy life, and some stories were not fit for company. But Mama didn't see the joy that lit poor Spencer's face when around his old acquaintances. They'd survived a hard life together, which bonded them in ways he could never bond with his parents or four younger sisters. Sometimes she sensed a wistfulness in him that she knew could not be satiated by this new life their family lived.

She patted her mother's hand. "I will find him, Mama." The dance and her partner had put her in such spirits, she couldn't refuse humoring her older brother.

Holly left her parents' amusement to Mr. Pelham and joined Spencer. As he finished his conversation, she glanced around the room to see if anyone of importance had arrived during the dance. Bath was quiet this time of year, but several older dignitaries often traveled to take the waters for their health. Sometimes they brought attractive companions with them, and Holly always made sure introductions were made.

She shook the thought from her head. Attractive companions didn't draw her in anymore. She'd almost forgotten.

Her eyes fell on a lone gentleman resting in a chair in the corner. The young man, probably Spencer's age, wore a dark blue coat with white lapels and gold buttons—a lieutenant's coat. His legs extended lazily before him. Well, what was left of them. A length of leather poked out from under the cuff of his breeches, with a wooden foot attached to the leather. Holly looked away so she wouldn't stare.

How lucky they were Spencer hadn't come home looking just like that. The thought made her stomach ache. They called him back to Gloucestershire soon after the war with the French began.

"Ah, there you are, Holly." Her brother turned from his conversation.

"Tell me, who has caught your eye tonight, Spencer?" she asked, leaning in conspiratorially. "I shall have Mama invite them all to dine."

Spencer shook his head with a wry grin. "You think that because you are engaged, you should marry off everyone in the room?"

"No, only the ones with wealth and position."

It didn't draw a laugh, as she'd hoped. Instead, Spencer's smile faded. "Come, I wish you to meet a dear friend of mine." Her brother caught her arm and steered her over to the wounded gentleman, and Holly stifled a sigh. Of course this sorry man was her brother's friend. The man got awkwardly to his feet as they approached.

"Holly, this is Lieutenant Brenton," Spencer said.

Lieutenant Brenton's straight, sand-colored hair was brushed to the side as though he hadn't spent more than seconds at the mirror. He did have a nice smile, she would admit to that. If not for his disfiguration, he could have stolen several hearts that night. Still, she hoped someday he would find happiness. Perhaps some spinster or other disgraced young lady could overlook the foot.

"I owe my life to Brenton, you know," Spencer went on. "He saved me from drowning when I fell off the dock just after I joined. And he taught me to swim after that so he wouldn't have to keep saving me."

The lieutenant threw back his head in laughter. The corners of Holly's lips tugged upward at the contagious sound. She extended her hand to him.

"How good it is to meet you, sir."

He took the proffered hand in a firm grip and bowed over it. "Likewise, Miss Addison. I was just watching you in the set. You are a lovely dancer."

Holly dropped her gaze, as a modest girl should do, and flashed him a smile.

A mischievous twinkle touched his green eyes. "This isn't the Miss Addison who nearly fainted dead away when we visited your home in Bristol, is it?"

Holly snatched her hand back. How dare he mention that place! After all they had done to cut ties with their former life. Now she vaguely remembered Spencer bringing the light-haired lieutenant home.

"Oh, yes," Spencer said. "I forgot you and Jacobson visited on our leave. How long ago was that? Six years? Seven?"

"Long enough that little Miss Addison's heart couldn't handle two dashing officers walking through her door."

Heat raged over Holly's skin. Her fingers found the fan hanging from her wrist, and she clutched it with all her strength. This sailor had no right to ridicule her, especially not here. How many people around them had heard his loud teasing?

"Even at fourteen," she said through clenched teeth, "I was not so much of a ninny as to faint over anyone lower in rank than a captain. I have my standards, sir."

She spun on her heel. Perhaps her mother was right in her opinion of Spencer's friends. She flounced over to her parents and Mr. Pelham, Lieutenant Brenton's chuckle following her all the way back.

Robert pushed a chair to the window of his small room. The floor below rattled with the rowdiness of the inn's other patrons. It was loud enough Robert wouldn't be able to sleep, though he didn't mind. Sleep wasn't always peaceful for him.

Darkness pervaded the little apartment, broken by patches of light from the street lamps outside. Robert sat, his hands instantly going to his leg. The ache had one solution. He didn't need light to unfasten the buckle and let the wooden foot drop to the floor.

A sigh escaped him, as it did every night. If only removing the foot took away all of the discomfort in his leg. What he'd give to swim in the sea, as he often did in Gibraltar to loosen the tension. In those days he had nurtured the crazy belief that if he kept up his strength, he could remain useful to the navy. The decision to leave had not come easily. The navy would have retained him as long as he wished for tedious shore duties, of course, but he'd eventually had enough. Though he hadn't received his official discharge papers yet, that chapter of his life was as good as closed.

Robert pulled out his flageolet, the little wooden flute an Irish carpenter aboard the HMS *Andersen* had given him. That was after Trafalgar. His fingers moved over the holes, coaxing out the haunting melody he had first learned while stuck in the belly of a ship trying to fathom the new life of limited mobility before him.

He stared through the window at the unhindered people walking by as he played. His father was right; getting away from all this humanity would do him good. Robert hadn't expected his father's letter that morning, nor had he expected his father to gift him Rowant. Not when it was his stepmother's sanctuary from Society. Robert could understand why she preferred it. The quiet West Country manor now called to him. Perhaps there he would find peace as well.

In the street below, a carriage pulled up. A gentleman stepped down, bowing and tipping his hat to whomever remained inside. Robert stopped playing and watched the man. A moment later, a head popped out of the coach door. Lamplight reflected off her flaxen hair.

Robert leaned forward. The giggle confirmed his suspicion—Miss Addison. Robert could just see her brother's silhouette through the carriage window, but it appeared no one else rode with them. Addison had mentioned his sister's engagement and that her intended was staying at this very inn.

Mr. Pelham pushed forward until his lips met hers. Moonlight glowed on her glove as her arm slid around his neck.

Robert tore his eyes away, and not because he was appalled. After what he'd seen of her at the ball, he'd expect nothing less from Miss Addison. He did not judge the lovers for a stolen kiss in the street. Heavens knew he'd seen worse in his navy days. He brought the flute to his lips and took up the tune again, slower and more resolute.

He envied them, for they had something he knew he would never have.

Robert leaned back in his chair. He wasn't in the little room in Bath any longer, but alone in a hammock that swayed with the ship's rocking. Behind him lay the world. Ahead . . .

He didn't quite know.

Holly pierced the delicate hem of a morning cap with her needle and pulled the fine thread through. No one would examine such an article at close range, but that didn't stop her from proceeding with the utmost care. She would know if a stitch were amiss, and she didn't want the first years of her marriage plagued with the knowledge she had failed a stitch on her morning cap.

The work kept her mind occupied from the fact that Mr. Pelham hadn't called since before the ball.

Holly bit the inside of her lip, trying to force down the twisting inside. It didn't mean anything. Even though he always called as early as socially acceptable the morning after a ball. He'd done that since before their engagement. And now it had been four days without a word.

Even Mama couldn't sit still. She paced before the window, then found her way to the fireplace, sat down to work on a project, then returned to the window. Her movement only prodded Holly's nerves.

Her mother sat, hands clasped before her. "Perhaps we should call for tea."

Before Holly could answer, a tap on the door brought both ladies' heads around. The butler entered.

"Mr. Pelham to see you."

Mama flew to her feet. "Send him in. And find Mr. Addison. Thank you." She clapped her hands together and shot Holly a smile. "You see? I told you everything would be fine."

Holly threw the cap into her basket, not bothering to secure the needle. It tapped against the side of the basket as it slid down through her projects to the bottom. Something to fret over later. She stood, then thought better of it and sat again. Her face warmed enough on its own that she didn't need to pinch her cheeks before his entrance.

Her father entered with Mr. Pelham, and the ladies rose. The man looked from Papa to Mama, an odd expression in his deep eyes that Holly could not explain.

"Mr. Pelham," her mother began, "won't you-"

"I've come on unpleasant business, Mrs. Addison," Mr. Pelham said with a curt bow. "I wish to delay it no further."

Holly's breath caught. What unpleasant business could so amiable a man as Mr. Pelham have with her family? Or perhaps it was unpleasant business with his own family, and he was forced to bring it to their attention? Would it delay the wedding? Holly swallowed. For the love of all things holy, she prayed it would not.

The gentleman cleared his throat. "I am withdrawing from the engagement previously arranged between myself and Miss Addison."

The words didn't make sense. Holly's hands flew to her stomach as the room started to spin. Mama cried out. Holly couldn't hear the words her mother's pleading voice rained on Mr. Pelham.

Withdrawing?

As though from a business deal he suddenly found undesirable.

Holly sank to the sofa, ripping her gaze from his emotionless eyes. She couldn't understand. He was breaking off the engagement?

"Confound it, man. What is the meaning of this?" her father snapped.

"I no longer desire the attachment."

Holly stared at the rug. But they were perfect for each other. What about their plans for the life they would share?

Papa's voice raised with each sentence he spoke. "You know what this will do to her. What of her reputation? Have you no honor?"

Her mother stood rooted to the floor, watching the gentlemen's exchange with wide eyes.

"I don't think this action of mine will have any effect on her reputation, and I sever the engagement in an attempt to salvage mine."

Holly slowly lifted her head. Mr. Pelham would not look at her. The shock within melted into bubbling, molten words that spewed from her lips as she rose and whirled.

"How dare you imply something amiss with my reputation, sir." She clenched her hands, feeling the steam swell inside. "I have been nothing but loyal since before the arrangement, and I wish to know what accusations you have against me. What foul gossip has reached your ears? Have out with it."

Mr. Pelham's eyebrow twitched, but he otherwise gave no reaction. "It is not so much what I have heard, but what I have observed myself in Society. Your unguarded interactions, your shameless flirtations have made me of a mind that you are not what I thought you to be. I do not think us a compatible match."

Holly sputtered before she could form a response. Flirtations! As though he didn't also flirt with every female in the room. He flirted with her own mother, for pity's sake.

She opened her mouth to tell him so, but he rushed on. "I have not come to argue the matter, only to inform you of my decision. All further concerns may be addressed to my attorney."

The tails of his coat flew out behind him as he exited, leaving the Addison family in silence in the drawing room. No one moved. They could only watch the door where Mr. Pelham had disappeared.

Part of Holly wept, hoping he would reappear and proclaim his display was all a good joke. The Mr. Pelham she knew wouldn't do this to her. He wanted her, and the grand life they were to have together.

But the gentle side of her heart did not usually win the day. In moments such as these, the stronger portion—beat into firmness in their years of poverty—took over.

Holly stormed from the room, not sure where she was going. Somewhere she could scream without disturbing her frazzled parents.

Her only consolation was that Spencer had taken the girls out walking. It meant her siblings didn't have to witness her dream castle come crashing down about her ears, leaving her standing in a pile of rubble and wasted hopes.

Chapter Two

Robert stretched his right leg as far out as he dared in the mail coach. Perhaps he should have taken up his father's offer of the carriage, but it was more economical to ride post, and he would have had to wait for the carriage to arrive from Wiltshire. He tried to distract himself from the ache of travel in his leg by staring out the window at the passing Cornish countryside.

He vividly remembered the last time he'd seen Cornwall. As a wide-eyed nine-year-old setting off for adventure, he hadn't understood all he was leaving behind. He saw his mother's tears and the white handkerchief she waved from the steps of Rowant Manor, the house they'd lived in until Father inherited the Aston Park Estate. He hadn't dreamed that one day his father would give him the house and its land.

It wasn't much of a living, hardly 700 pounds per annum. But after seventeen years at sea, the last two of them keeping books at a port in the

Mediterranean while he mended, Robert didn't know if he could actually manage a house, land, and tenants. Even for a property so small as Rowant.

Across from him sat two women who hadn't spoken a word since he got in the coach at the inn a few hours ago. The first, plump with silver spirals poking from her bonnet, gave him a kindly smile on his entrance. The second didn't acknowledge him and conspicuously kept the hood of her cloak pulled down to conceal her face. The travel dress underneath was a simple blue, but looked well made.

Robert twiddled his fingers over an imaginary flute, itching to break the silence in the carriage. He had avoided social visits and small talk since he'd returned to England a few weeks ago. The ball last week was his first in years. But even in his solitude he didn't appreciate the lack of noise.

"Lovely weather today," he said, nodding to the sunny sky outside the window.

"That it is, sir," the older woman said, glancing at her companion. "Wouldn't you say so, Miss Addison?"

Addison's sister? Of all people to meet on the road, surely he wouldn't meet her. Robert leaned forward, trying to catch a glimpse of the lady's face. "Miss Holly Addison?" Why was she here, practically alone? And in a mail coach.

She finally looked up, her large gray eyes rimmed with red. His heart gave a curious flip.

Miss Addison flinched at the sight of him and locked her gaze on the window. Clearly she still hadn't forgiven him for his joke at the ball.

But Robert wouldn't give up that easily.

"Where are you headed, Miss Addison?" Her brother hadn't mentioned the family quitting Bath. "And Mrs . . ."

"Phelps," the older woman said. "My master and mistress have sent us to Cornwall."

"Sent us!" Miss Addison tore her gaze from the window to glare at her servant. "They exiled us to some forsaken village. Heaven forbid they keep a disgraced daughter in their presence."

"Now, miss, you know it wasn't like that," Mrs. Phelps said, eyes wide after her mistress's outburst. She lowered her voice as though to keep him from hearing, an impossible feat in such close quarters. The young lady pulled her hand away from the servant's attempts to soothe her. "They didn't want you to have to face the gossip."

Interest piqued, Robert sat back to listen to their conversation play out. When last he'd seen her, Miss Addison had been the envy of all. How had she fallen so far in so short a time?

"I will face it now, or I will face it later," Miss Addison hissed. Her voice was tight, as though holding back tears. She didn't attempt to lower her voice as the servant had. "I am ruined either way."

Robert didn't know what pushed him to speak— the love of his friend, or his sudden interest in this young lady, so out of his reach. "Surely it's not so bad as that."

Miss Addison slumped against the coach's wall, hands limp in her lap. "But it is, Lieutenant."

"What happened?" He rested his elbows on his knees, ignoring the pang it sent through his leg.

The young lady hesitated, eyes searching his face. He wondered what she saw there. A wounded, broken man? Someone she could trust? A friend?

"Mr. Pelham has called off our engagement. He says I have not been," she swallowed, "faithful."

Robert scowled. He hardly knew the Addison family save the son, but they seemed respectable. A bit haughty, perhaps, but not dishonorable. And no one who saw her interacting with that pompous dandy at the ball could question her devotion to the relationship. "On what grounds?"

She shook her head, ringlets fluttering about her face. The hood of her cloak had crept back, but she made no move to restore its position. "I have been true, I swear it. I don't know what it is he saw that led him to his conclusion. And now my parents have banished me to live with my father's half-sister."

"I am so sorry." He didn't know how it felt to fall from the good graces of Society. He had never really been in its good graces. But he did know the paralyzing fear of having a bright future pulled out from under him, and he knew the pain of finding himself utterly alone in a world where he used to thrive.

She gave him a puzzled look. "Why do you care so much? You don't even like Society."

Robert cocked his head and chuckled. "What gave you that impression?"

"At the ball you sulked in the corner instead of dancing."

"You are mistaken, Miss Addison. I love to dance, and once I could rival even one so talented as you on the floor." He flashed her a smile to discourage his own feelings as much as anything.

"Why did you stop?" Her eyebrow arched.

Robert rapped his right boot against the floor of the carriage, the hit letting out a solid and inhuman thud. "After Trafalgar, I didn't have a choice."

Miss Addison sank back, eyes wide as she stared at his boot concealing the false foot. Robert let the conversation dissolve. They rode in silence until they reached Liskeard. He helped her down from the coach, but she wouldn't meet his eyes. He assisted Mrs. Phelps, then helped the coachman remove his and the ladies' trunks.

"Good day to you," he said with a tip of his hat, then limped away as she mumbled her thanks.

He wished her well. He truly did. But his head was clouded with hopes of things that could never be, with her or any woman, and it was best to put distance between them.

Darkness had set in by the time Holly and Mrs. Phelps reached the manor. A part of her hoped Aunt Margaret had gone to bed early, even though it was barely time for dinner. She didn't want to see anyone tonight, especially not after seeing Lieutenant Brenton in the coach that morning.

The wheels of the hired coach retreated across the gravely path behind them. Lamps near the door reflected off the half-timbered house's plastered sides, giving the building an unnatural glow. Holly couldn't fathom why her aunt had chosen to visit this ancient house when her new husband had a comfortable estate in Wiltshire. The squat manor before her brought to mind her childhood home in Bristol. Only this house was bigger.

Aunt Margaret hadn't gone to bed. She met Holly at the door, her dark hair pulled up in a simple knot. "It is good to see you. How was the journey?" She wrung her hands, as though she didn't know what else to do with them.

Holly pushed down the tears as she thought on every solitary mile she'd crossed since leaving Bath. "We had no troubles."

"You've grown so much since I last saw you." The woman's tight voice barely carried over the sounds of servants unloading the hired coach.

"I should hope so. I was only twelve." Holly glanced around the vestibule. If it could be called that. Low wooden beams crossed the ceiling in stately lines, darkening the hallway that bled into a tiny sitting room. Past the sofas she could see the dining room, crowded with a simple table and chairs. Wooden stairs led up to a second floor that couldn't hold more than five bedrooms.

This was where her parents intended her to stay?

"Are you hungry? I'm afraid I take simple meals, but the cook does her job well. I was just about to sit down."

"Oh, no. Thank you. I . . . I think I need rest more than anything." Holly wanted nothing more than to close her eyes and block out this horrid house.

Aunt Margaret put a timid hand on her shoulder. "I'll send up a tray, in case you change your mind."

"No, I truly am not hungry. Thank you." She said it more forcefully than she meant to. Her aunt nodded and backed away, eyes lowered. Holly might have felt sorry if she had any place left inside. Too many other emotions had taken up residence.

The maid showed Holly to her room, where her trunk already sat. Mrs. Phelps came in to help her undress, but Holly shooed her away. She didn't want the lady's maid, who was far too old for the position anyhow, hovering about her like a governess. She wanted to be alone. If only Mama had fired Mrs. Phelps when she found a younger woman for the position, instead of insisting Holly take her.

Holly drifted around the unadorned room which was to be her new home. She tried to reassure herself that it wouldn't be permanent. Aunt Margaret would return to Wiltshire eventually, and perhaps Mama would send for her before then. She only had to be patient.

A little watercolor hung on the wall, the only decoration in the room. Four little faces watched her from the frame. Three brown-haired children wore tight jackets, while the smallest had a white infant's gown. Wispy yellow hair, touched with the faintest hint of red, circled its cherubic face. The painting faded into pencil lines that belied its unfinished state.

She touched the wood frame, bitterness swelling in her chest. In a few years, perhaps she would have made her own painting of a brood of little Pelhams. How could that future be gone?

Holly turned her back on the painting and threw herself onto the bed, not bothering to change. What did it matter now? No one cared what she did—not her parents, not her siblings, not Mr. Pelham.

Chapter Three

Perhaps Robert shouldn't have made the extra stop on his journey to visit his former comrade. His leg would agree with that assessment. Robert bid farewell to his friend's coachman, who'd been good enough to carry his trunk up the stairs to Rowant Manor's door. Robert could mostly manage the trunk, but stairs were his weakness. With the state of his leg just now, he didn't think he would have made it.

No lights shone from the house. His stepmother, who had retired to Rowant for her health, must have thought he would stay the night with his friend. He had told her to expect him tonight, but he supposed most people didn't travel so late.

He fumbled with the door, grateful for the full moon's light behind him. It creaked open, and the familiar scent of old wood hit him. It drew out his smile, and he paused on the threshold, breathing it deeply. Perhaps here he could reclaim a semblance of the man he was before Trafalgar.

Though stealth was not his strongpoint these days, Robert took care to close the door quietly. He'd send for a servant in the morning to bring the trunk to his room. He didn't want to wake his stepmother. Gerald said the poor woman's nerves, more than anything, had been to blame for her removing to Cornwall. Robert had only met her a few times, as his father remarried during one of his assignments, but she did seem an anxious lady.

Robert pulled himself up the stairs. He didn't need a light to make his way to his old room. A surge of nostalgia washed through him as he shuffled down the hall, trailing his fingers along the walls. He stopped before his room and turned the handle. It stuck, just as it always had, before popping open.

His throat constricted. The light of the moon fell in the middle of the room, about the spot where his mother had knelt the morning of his departure for the navy. Little did he know it was the last time he'd see her face. Robert had mourned her passing when word reached the *Andersen*, but a third-rate ship of the line was an easy place to forget sorrows.

Now, as he stared at the floor, a tear slipped through his defenses. It fell from his face, and in the quiet of the night he heard it hit his boot. What would she think of that boot and the false foot it concealed? His heart whispered that she wouldn't see it. She'd only see her son.

Blinking to keep back the rest of the emotion, Robert closed the door and crossed to the bed. It creaked as he sat. A whiff of lavender tickled his nose. Just like the lavender water his mother used to wear. The maid must have sprinkled it on the bed linens to freshen them. It was the perfect touch for this memory-filled evening. Now he only needed toy soldiers strewn across the floor to make him believe he had stepped back into his childhood.

Time to relieve the pressure that coursed up his leg. He tugged off his boots and rolled up the leg of his trousers. His fingers found the buckle that held the blasted foot on. In moments, the tension eased. He let the foot clomp to the floor.

The bed moved behind him. Before he could wonder at its source, a shriek pierced his ears. He shot off of the bed and tried to pivot on the missing foot. His arms grasped wildly for something to steady himself as he hurtled backward. Air whistled through his fingers.

He cracked his head against floor, and a string of curses burst from his mouth. Who the blazes was in his room?

"Get out!" The shrill voice echoed through the room. "Get out!"

The door flew open, revealing his stepmother in her dressing gown. A little candle illuminated her pale face. She looked from Robert on the floor to the bed, and a hand came to her face.

"Merciful heavens," she cried. "Robert, are you hurt? I didn't think you would arrive until tomorrow."

Robert groaned as he rolled to his knees, his head throbbing in time with his leg. "Who is that?"

He crawled to the wall for support while he stood. Wide eyes peeked out from under the blankets on his bed.

"I apologize." His stepmother's voice came out in gasps. "It is my niece. I received word she would be coming just after I heard from your father, and I did not think a letter would reach you in time to tell you."

"But why is she in my room?" Robert leaned into the wall, rubbing his head. He took a deep breath. No need to frighten the woman more, to say nothing of the girl on the bed who was no doubt terrified to find a strange man in the room. He kept his eyes trained on his stepmother. Who knew what state of dress the girl was in?

"I—I thought you would take the master's room. I am so sorry, Robert."

He fabricated a smile for her. "No harm done. But if you would retrieve my leg, I'll be on my way to the other bedroom." So much for spending the night wrapped in memories of former days. He had hardly entered his father's room when they lived here before.

His stepmother scurried across the room, and the light of her candle caught the mess of golden curls belonging to the niece on the bed. The young lady's mouth dropped open.

"Lieutenant Brenton?"

Robert let his head fall back against the wall and closed his eyes. Then he laughed, for he didn't know what else to do. "Miss Addison, a pleasure to see you again."

Holly lay in bed after they'd gone, mind whirling from Lieutenant Brenton's intrusion. She didn't know her father's half-sister well, and it had slipped her mind that Aunt Margaret's new surname was Brenton. How had she not made the connection?

Though she knew it shouldn't, the presence of that gentleman in her place of exile sent prickles up her arms. He must be so pleased to see her humbled after how she responded to his teasing at the ball.

Except in the mail coach she hadn't seen any smugness in his features. He had listened intently, with unfeigned remorse. And despite his injury had helped her from the carriage. He hadn't treated her like the disgraced lady her parents saw.

Holly curled up under the blankets. She'd left her gown and stays in a heap on the floor, but had locked the door to prevent further interruptions to her needed sleep. Now the sleep wouldn't come.

The little voice of a flute drifted through the blackness inside the house. Holly raised her head. Its sad notes whispered through the door, pulling at her heart, singing of loneliness and fear. Her head sank back down to the pillow. She didn't know the song, and yet she thought she could sing along. It touched her so sharply, she didn't even consider going to her aunt to make the upstart servant stop.

Holly wiped at the wetness coursing down her cheeks, praying for the oblivion of sleep to help heal her smarting soul.

Chapter Four

Nearly a week of moping and keeping mostly to her room had stirred something inside Holly. She would soon go mad if she walked the barren bedroom any more. Exploring the house did little to amuse her. In ten minutes she had seen the whole of it—library, bedrooms, and all. The garden could hardly claim the title. She'd trudged back to her room after seeing Rowant's meager offerings.

Except the master bedroom, of course. She avoided that spot of the house. Rarely had she met the lieutenant during the day, and she intended to keep it that way. Even now, pacing her little room, her cheeks burned at the humiliating mistake the night of their arrivals. Praise heaven she had fallen asleep in her gown before the lieutenant burst in. She pressed her hands to her eyes, but couldn't blot out the sight of his shocked face staring at her in the darkness. If she'd let Mrs. Phelps do her duty, the scene could have been much worse.

Her breakfast tray sat practically untouched on the desk. It hadn't taken long for the silent breakfasts downstairs to bore her. Lieutenant Brenton ate long before the ladies, a bowl of gruel and cup of tea according to Aunt Margaret, and was off on business before she even woke. Despite the awkwardness she felt each time he looked at her with that hidden smirk, she wished he would eat a little later to help combat the dullness.

Holly closed the curtains to block out the incessant morning sunlight. She couldn't stay here. Her parents hadn't intended her to live like this again. But how could she convince them to send for her?

Holly sat at the small desk, pushed aside the tray, and pulled out paper and her pen. She would write to them. If only she could conjure the words that would make them call her home.

Curse Mr. Pelham and his ridiculous imaginings! If it weren't for him, she'd still be comfortably situated in her parent's residence in Bath.

She paused in the midst of opening her ink bottle, lips pursing.

Mr. Pelham.

He had forced her into this, and he could save her from it. If she could change his mind, convince him his worries were unfounded, would he take her back? Her parents would send for her in the blink of an eye. Perchance even move up the wedding date in their joy of the whole scandal getting resolved.

Holly dipped her pen, her hand trembling in excitement. Yes, Mr. Pelham would save her. He was perhaps the only one who could save her.

7 October 1807
Rowant Manor, Cornwall

My dearest Miles,
It seems a lifetime since I last saw you. I will forever treasure the memory of our final dance and the last kiss when we parted that night.
Sweet Miles, tell me it isn't gone forever.

Holly breathed, fighting to control her penmanship. They would forget this misunderstanding once they married. It would all be a good joke. And all would be right again.

If she hurried, she could send it to the post office with a servant in time for the mail coach. Surely her heartfelt words would convince Mr. Pelham, and she could be back within the week. The thought buoyed her sunken spirits. She could endure Rowant and Cornwall for another week.

Robert didn't know what the lad's mother had been thinking when she named him Broom. Perhaps the efforts of childbirth had clouded her judgment.

He watched the young man—who worked as footman, stablehand, and whatever else was needed at Rowant—adjust the hinges on the door of the stables.

"Perhaps when the harvest is brought in, we can clear land for a garden. Then we'd have less work in the spring."

Broom made no comment.

"What do you think of that?" Robert prodded.

"Whatever you like, sir."

He glanced back at the house and surrounding land, which was mostly yellowing grass. The dry year hadn't done it any favors. "If my stepmother is to reside at Rowant on a frequent basis, I should think she would like a garden to walk through."

"Yes, sir."

Robert frowned. "Don't you have an opinion?"

The boy lifted his curly head. "Can't say I know much about gardens."

"Can't say I do, either." Robert scratched under his jaw. Owning land was a bothersome business. At sea, he always knew his duty and when to do it. Here . . .

"Lieutenant Brenton, I've been looking for you." Miss Addison sauntered around the side of the stable, skirts held up to prevent her hems dragging in the dirt. Slender boots, no doubt the latest style, stuck out beneath the soft material.

He stepped away from Broom, dusting off his coat. "How may I be of service, Miss Addison?"

She met his gaze with a sharp look. "I am looking for a servant to take this letter to the post office. My aunt couldn't spare any of the house servants. Can that young man be spared?"

"Broom? No, he has work at the house as well after this."

Her full lips pulled into a pout, and he had to admit it a pretty one. He fought with a smile. "Perhaps someone could take it later, or tomorrow."

"No, it must go out today," she said, hands curling into fists at her sides. The letter crinkled between her fingers.

Robert clutched his lapels, setting his face with a proud smirk. "Well, miss, I know of someone who can take it."

Miss Addison stepped forward. "You do? Who?"

He dipped his head toward her, catching once more the scent of lavender water.

"You."

Storm clouds raced across her gray eyes. "I do not appreciate your humor, sir."

Robert laughed softly and returned to inspect the door. Broom had finished the job well. At least, it seemed that way. He didn't have much knowledge on the fixing of doors.

"Anything else, Lieutenant Brenton?" the boy asked.

"Yes, will you hitch one of the horses to the cart?"

The young man nodded and hurried into the stable.

Robert rested his shoulder against the wall. Miss Addison hadn't moved, but her eyes shot daggers at him.

"What is the importance of this letter that it cannot wait until tomorrow?" He held out his hand. "To whom do you write?"

Miss Addison pulled it in to her chest and turned away. "That is none of your concern."

He raised his hands. So protective of a letter. But he shouldn't judge. The young lady no doubt missed her friends and family. Her former intended.

Ah, yes. The letter couldn't be to anyone else. He opened his mouth to make a joke, but the words balked on his tongue. He wouldn't win any ground with Miss Addison if he continued to tease.

"Come, I will take you to Portholland." He held out his arm to her.

"On that leg?"

He snorted. "No, I thought to borrow four better ones."

Bless his father for teaching him to drive a cart early in his childhood. With Miss Addison situated beside him, Robert turned the cart and thick farm horse onto the Portholland road. The reins felt foreign in his hands, too flimsy compared to the thick rope of the HMS *Andersen*.

They reached the village in no time, the clear sky chasing away whatever October chill had tried to set in that morning. Little houses and shops dotted the street where villagers called out greetings to each other. Fishermen's families sold the early catch, and a hunched old woman steered a tinkling pushcart down the road. Seeing the white-haired woman made the corner of his mouth tick upward. After all these years, she still walked the streets of Portholland. At least one thing hadn't changed.

Miss Addison stared at the pushcart as they descended. Bright sun glinted off the seller's wares, so much Robert could hardly tell the shape, though he knew exactly what the bangles were.

"They sell silver trinkets here?" Miss Addison asked, following the old woman.

The seller swiveled her head back. "Interested, miss?" The pushcart stopped, necklaces clinking together. Below the swaying jewelry lay a collection of more useful utensils, plates, and cups.

"Myttin da," Robert said to the woman, dragging up the Cornish greeting she'd taught him years ago. It earned him a grateful nod. "As a matter of fact, it's tin. Lovely, isn't it?"

Almost as lovely as the picture Miss Addison made, reaching up a delicate hand to stroke the shining jewelry. If someone wished to entice Society to visit the seaside village, they could get no better image. Her hand came to rest under a little heart on a simple chain.

"How could an ugly metal like tin make something so beautiful?" she murmured. The light seemed caught in the pendant, reflecting back into her eyes and chasing away the earlier clouds.

He moved to her side to examine it with her. "Sometimes we don't know something's true beauty until it has been put through the fire by a master craftsman."

Her hand dropped down. "Why go through the trouble to change it? Was the tin not good enough to begin with?" She squinted, but he didn't think because of the brightness about them.

Robert tapped the heart, sending it spinning. Its reflected light splashed across the other items in the cart and made everything sparkle. "Look what it has become. Something far more grand than it imagined."

Miss Addison looked away, then dug into her reticule and brought the square of paper out. She tried to conceal the address, but Robert saw enough of it to confirm his suspicions. She was begging the man to return to her.

Poor woman.

"The post office, Lieutenant?"

He pointed, and she hurried off without looking back. He imagined her curls, now concealed beneath her bonnet, bouncing as they had the night of the ball. Someday she would find a man who appreciated her, not her name or position or dowry. He wished she would not give up hope.

"Anything for the lady, me'ansome?" the old woman asked, a mischievous twinkle in her eye.

Robert watched Miss Addison disappear into the post office. He couldn't hope for something more than friendship, but perhaps friendship was what the young lady needed just now.

He nodded and fished out a coin.

Holly wondered how far her letter had made it as she climbed into bed that night.

Lieutenant Brenton's bed.

Her cheeks flared. Thank goodness Mrs. Phelps had retired already, so as not to see the reaction. Besides, he hadn't slept there since he was a young boy. He'd told her the entire story on their way back from Portholland, of how he left and sought his fortune on the seas at his father's suggestion. His older brother James had already joined the navy. She'd seen the regret in his eyes when talking of Captain Brenton recently receiving command of a ship.

It was the same regret she saw in Spencer's eyes. Both were forced out of their familiar world, though Spencer met a much better fate than Lieutenant Brenton.

Holly looked around the room, pausing at the little watercolor of the children. The little baby must have been Lieutenant Brenton. She giggled, imagining his firm cheekbones once concealed by those luscious baby cheeks. What a pity he'd lost the red tint to his sandy hair.

She pulled the blankets around her and hugged her knees in. He'd made his story interesting, at least. She hadn't laughed in so many days.

Holly didn't want to concede how much she'd enjoyed it.

She lay down, and her face knocked something hard nestled in her pillow. What on earth? She fished it out and held it up. In the waning light of the candle beside her bed, the tin heart from the peddler glowed, and a deep, hidden spot in her own heart followed suit. She couldn't account for such a forward gesture as buying her trinkets. Mr. Pelham had never done that for her, and they had been engaged.

Somewhere in the house, the flute's gentle voice came to life. It started its usual melancholy sighing, but after a few moments paused. Then it took up a hesitantly merrier tune. Holly placed the necklace beside the candle and snuffed out the flame, the image of the little heart still pulsing in her vision.

Chapter Five

13 October 1807
Rowant Manor, Cornwall

My dearest Miles,

Your silence pains my tender heart. Would that I could convince you of my deepest devotion. What token would you have of me? All that is mine I willingly give to you and beg you to accept it. My dear, tell me what rumors you heard, what you saw. I wish so desperately to mend this chasm between us.

The days have dragged on, with no light on my horizon nor stars to ease the darkness of night. I dream only of your embrace, weeping at the thought that I may never feel the strength of your arms around me again.

These people with whom I reside have not your sense of excitement, nor the perfect style I so admire in you. My aunt and her stepson content themselves with a life of solitude which I cannot comprehend. Surely you are of the same mind, that the company of one's friends and family are the greatest pleasure in life.

My darling, I plead with you not to leave me to this sorry fate, brought on by such misunderstanding. My heart remains yours. It always has, and I know always shall.

Your devoted love,
H. Addison

Holly grumbled her way down the stairs, another letter clutched in her hand. It had been a week since she sent the first letter, and no word from Mr. Pelham. Why hadn't he left Bath immediately on its reception and come to her aid? Perhaps she hadn't put enough sincerity into her words.

Well, if that was the case, surely this new letter would convince him. She spotted the young servant walking through the hall with a pair of boots to clean.

"You there."

The young man glanced up at her with thick lowered brows. "Miss?"

She held up the letter. "Go directly to the village to post this."

"I have—"

"Make haste!" She shoved the square into his hands. He took it with a sigh. Clearly not one of the polished servants she was used to in Bath. If she were mistress of this house, he would not work there long. "What is your name, boy?" She would bring the lieutenant's attention to this unacceptable behavior. Whenever she could find him.

"Broom Driver," he growled, and stomped from the hall.

No, he would definitely not be employed long in a house she ran.

Holly swept into the dining room. She had considered sending for a tray, as she did many mornings. How embarrassing to have to breakfast in the dining room when not residing in London. She'd seen many townhouses larger than this manor. She curtsied to her aunt, who took up her usual position at the head of the small table and was spreading cream on a roll. How many couples could it seat? Four, if they packed themselves in?

"Good morning, Aunt Margaret."

"Good morning, Miss Addison," a deeper, playful voice answered.

Lieutenant Brenton sat at the opposite end as his stepmother, his usual brilliant grin brightening the heavy room. How could he keep that smile on his face at so early an hour? It couldn't be half past nine. But then, she didn't understand how he smiled at all in his situation.

"It has not been a good morning for me, Lieutenant, but I am grateful for your concern." Holly sat, feeling him watching her movement. Why did it send a strange quiver through her? "How kind of you to grace us with your presence this morning."

Aunt Margaret chewed on her lip as she poured tea for Holly. "I hope you slept well," she said softly.

"I did not sleep well at all." Holly plucked a cold piece of toast from a platter and nibbled on it. She missed the grand spreads from Bath. This reminded her of Bristol.

"Thinking too much of someone?" the lieutenant asked.

The bite of toast stuck in her throat. Holly fought to swallow it, washing it down with tea that burned her tongue. She wiped her mouth, flashing a frown in his direction. She had been thinking too much of someone, and it wasn't Mr. Pelham. Perhaps that was the cause of her foul mood this morning.

"I wasn't comfortable. The room was too cold."

"I know one gentleman who could fix that," Lieutenant Brenton muttered into his tea, green eyes glimmering with held-in laughter. "Have you received any good news from Bath?"

The irritated embers in her chest flared. Thanks to Spencer, she kept company with sailors often enough that his joke, if it could be called a joke, did not shock her. She expected nothing better than uncouth humor from a man of the sea. To bring up her former betrothed, and in the same breath suggest.

She ground her teeth.

"Robert," Aunt Margaret warned.

Holly jumped to her feet. "I believe it had to do with the puddle I found on my floor from last night's rain. Your decrepit house has a leak, sir. Probably more than one. I cannot believe the rotten luck that has put me in such a filthy place with someone so unfashionable and rude as you!"

And then she did something she would never have dared do in Bath. Hands moving of their own accord, she balled up her napkin and threw it at the lieutenant's jeering face. He dodged, but the useless cloth only made it to his bowl of gruel before falling limp with a squishing plop.

His eyes met hers. Heat drained from her face. How had she let this simpleton affect her so? His lips twitched.

She spun and ran from the room before his aggravating presence made her do anything worse. His rumbling chuckle rang in her ears as she fled, fuming.

She should have sent for a breakfast tray.

Robert smoothed the plaster over the offending crack near the roof of the house. It looked sloppy compared to Broom's work on other parts of the house, but he'd get it smooth. It would just take him longer. Like everything he attempted these days. And perhaps it would dispel some of Miss Addison's rage from that morning.

He knew he shouldn't have made the comments about Mr. Pelham. The voice in his head had whispered a warning. He shouldn't ignore that voice, especially where Miss Addison was concerned. Idiot.

Something about the way she drew herself straighter and jutted out her chin when offended amused him to no end. He hadn't found someone who intrigued him so much in a very long time. Perhaps ever. He hadn't been on land long enough in the last ten years to give anyone the chance.

The nearby window screeched open, and Robert didn't know whether to be pleased or worried, but he knew which of the two sentiments she would be.

Her blonde head popped through the window. "Lieutenant Brenton, what are you doing?"

"Fixing the leak that so vexed you this morning."

"You will fall and break your neck."

Robert glanced down at the ladder propped against the side of the house. He had his uninjured foot planted on one rung, the knee of his wounded leg on another for balance. His coat, cravat, and waistcoat lay discarded in the grass below.

"I've been in more precarious positions than this," he said with a shrug and returned to smoothing the plaster. He'd climbed all over ships in his days at sea.

"Before or after you lost your foot?"

He cocked his head. "Touché, Miss Addison."

"Why are you not having the Broom boy fix this? This is not work for a gentleman." Clear disgust cut through her voice.

Robert gave her what he hoped was a stern look. "Because someone sent the Broom boy to the post office this morning on important business, and I want this to have enough time to dry before the storm rolls in."

Miss Addison's eyes narrowed. "There's hardly a cloud in the sky."

"Do you see those little wisps on the eastern horizon? See the trails they make? There's a stiff wind blowing, and that often means storms." He turned on the ladder to point out the clouds.

The ladder raised off the wall at his movement, and his stomach lurched.

She yelped, grabbing for his arm just out of her reach. He shifted his weight and the ladder slapped back against the wall. Miss Addison kept her hand extended toward him.

"Be careful, Lieutenant!" The haughty temper from that morning had vanished. He would have made a joke of her trying to take his hand, if not for the real concern in her large eyes.

He hadn't seen that in a woman's eyes. Not since his mother on the day of his departure for Portsmouth.

She pulled her arm back slowly, then sank into her room and closed the window.

Robert returned to his task. His pulse raced.

And not from the near fall.

Chapter Six

Lieutenant Brenton had been right. A storm rolled in that afternoon and stayed for three days. Stuck inside as rain and wind beat down, Holly decided to work on her next letter to Mr. Pelham. She threw many pages into the fire for mistakes or bland words. One she had even addressed to the lieutenant, to her mortification. That one she watched at the hearth be sure it had completely crumbled into ashes.

After rereading the latest attempt, she dropped her pen to the desk and pushed back her chair. Ink bled from the pen onto the page beneath it. Why couldn't she write a silly letter?

The thunder masked her frustrated moan. It had combined with the rainstorm only this morning. At least it added some interest to the monotony of being forced inside.

As the rumble died out, the flute's voice greeted her ear. She perked up, turning toward the door. How strange. She never heard it during the day. Thunder punctured the haunting melody, but the flute kept on through the pounding. Like a bird flying against a stiff wind, or a boat on a raging sea.

Like Lieutenant Brenton did through all the difficulties he faced because of his wound. She'd seen him pause on the stairs, face creased with pain, before pulling himself the rest of the way up with the help of the railing. And she couldn't understand the way he smiled, even with weariness in his eyes.

Holly left her chair and wandered to the bed, where the little tin heart sat beside the candle. She remembered him talking about how he had loved to dance once. A story her brother told in a letter wriggled into her mind, of an assembly he'd attended soon after his advancement. One of his friends had danced every dance, putting every gentleman in attendance to shame. Had that been Lieutenant Brenton?

She picked up the necklace and fastened it around her neck. Its smooth coolness sent a tingle across her skin. She could not imagine dancing being taken from her. Not permanently. Being at Rowant Manor had taken away Bath's frequent balls and assemblies, but when Mr. Pelham came for her she would have them back again.

The lieutenant would never get it back.

Holly's gaze strayed to the window. The lieutenant moved about with surprising ease, considering his wound. He'd proven that while repairing the leak. Her stomach lurched at the memory of his near fall. If he'd plunged to his death trying to see to her comfort, would she ever have forgiven herself? Now she was in his debt, and it served her right after the scene she caused in the breakfast room just prior to the incident on the ladder.

She rubbed her brow, eyes squeezing closed. Had she truly thrown her napkin at him? Like a petulant girl unready to leave the nursery. Perhaps she could recompense him. But how, following such a blunder?

Holly tilted her head, considering. Surely there was a way Lieutenant Brenton could dance again. Yes, that was it. She dug through her repertoire of dances. So many complex steps he couldn't maneuver without two feet. But if they modified the steps . . . A slower tune, a little practice, and he could do quite well.

And she would prove him wrong about dancing while repaying his kindness. That thought brought a smirk to her face. He had bested her in most every conversation they'd had since her arrival. She couldn't wait to taste the sweetness of this victory.

Perhaps whatever servant played the flute could accompany them. No doubt it was that Broom boy, shirking his duties. But she couldn't fault him for it just then. He was part of her scheme.

Holly darted into the hallway in search of the lieutenant. The flute's song grew louder as she floated down the hall toward the house's small book room the lieutenant frequented. She tapped softly on the door and opened it.

Lieutenant Brenton stood at the window, his back to her. Rain pattered against the panes, which rattled when thunder exploded around them. The storm increased, pummeling the walls. He hadn't lit any candles. The faint light from the shrouded skies outlined his figure as he faced the gale.

He winced at every crack from the seething skies. His shoulders hunched each time lightning lit the room, as though bracing himself for the next blow. The tune that wove about the house never ceased.

Holly crept into the room, unable to look away. "Lieutenant?"

He turned. His usual grin was gone. A little fipple flute rested in his hands, his fingers over the holes.

Lieutenant Brenton played the melodies she fell asleep to every night?

"Are you all right, sir?" His face looked paler than she'd seen it. Almost fashionably pale, yet it worried her to see it on him.

"I will be well enough soon." He laughed, but she heard no mirth in it. "How pathetic am I, afraid of a little storm?"

Something hid behind his careless words.

Thunder roared, and he clenched his eyes shut. He lifted the flute to his lips. The song drifted out from the instrument, curling through the plinking on the window.

Holly moved to stand beside him. His brows drew together as he played. Strong fingers rose and fell along the length of the delicate flute. His weren't the hands of a gentleman. Would time ever wash away the roughness formed by a life at sea? Not if he continued to do things like repair the wall.

"What is it?" Her voice came out as a whisper. "Tell me, please."

He played through the end of the tune, then lowered the flute. "Every time . . ." He sighed, not looking at her. "It's ridiculous, but every time thunder hits, I'm back . . ."

Back? Where? Her eyes dropped to his foot, and a sharp stab shot through her heart.

"At Trafalgar," she finished for him.

He shook his head and let it fall to his hand. "I heard the crack of the Spanish cannon. I should have ducked back down the ladder. But I was shouting to the captain, and the next moment I was on the deck."

Holly's eyes stung. She imagined him writhing on the floor as explosions burst around him. Had someone been there to lift him? To reassure him all would be well?

"Did . . ." She licked her lips, not sure if she wanted to know. "Did it come off then?"

His head shook slowly. "It wasn't repairable. The surgeon took it off soon after."

Holly didn't know when her hand wrapped around his, which still gripped the little flute. She couldn't loosen his grasp if she tried with all the tension coursing through his hand. He seemed oblivious to her touch as scenes of war ran past his unseeing eyes.

How did he keep all of these memories inside, without so much as a hint they plagued him? How did he smile and laugh? Spencer had witnessed horrors, but not like this.

"I'd seen it happen to so many men. I never thought it would happen to me. Nor how difficult it would be to come back."

She squeezed his hand. "But you have come back. Wonderfully. Look how well you can move about. And no one would know you still struggle with the memories. You have a wonderful life here." It did seem to suit him, even if it didn't suit her. Some enjoyed the peace and solitude.

The corner of his mouth tugged upward, but when he looked at her those green eyes still pulsed with sorrow. "Not one I can share with anyone."

Her throat constricted, catching the breath in her chest. How could she have been so cruel to this man, who smiled to try to push the darkness away? She gently took the flute from his hand, her fingers trailing along his as though she could lift some of the weight he carried. His eyes followed the flute to where she placed it on the desk. He looked as though he wanted to snatch it up again and drown these feelings in song.

"Come with me," she said, taking his now empty hand.

It felt like an age before he broke his gaze away from the instrument. His fingers clutched hers when the skies thundered again. "Where are we going?"

She pulled on his hand with both of hers, and he followed her to the door. A strange excitement bubbled within, and she grinned. "To dance."

When they'd pushed the sofa and chairs to the edges of the drawing room and rolled up the rug, Robert turned to Miss Addison. "I think climbing a ladder is simpler than dancing, and you couldn't handle my doing that."

"Hush and come stand here." She scurried to one end of the room.

"Are we at the top or bottom of the set?" he asked.

She frowned over her shoulder. "Why does that matter, if we're the only couple?"

He shrugged. "I want to know if I'm dancing with the haughty Miss Addison or the humble Miss Addison." At the sight of her dropped jaw, a laugh burst from him, blocking out the boom of thunder and the scenes of carnage it carried.

"I am helping you, Lieutenant Brenton." She wagged a finger at him. "Remember that."

"Oh, I thought perhaps you needed something to occupy your time in this decrepit house."

She took his shoulders and firmly moved him into place across from her. "No more of that, sir. I am captain of this operation."

He straightened and gave her a mock salute, which won him a reluctant smile. What had gotten into her, he couldn't say, but she had just laughed at a tease. Or almost laughed. It had to count for something.

"Now, you bow. That is something you know you can do." She hummed the first few bars and curtsied while he bowed. "Step forward, then back." He followed her commands. His boots echoed against the floor. If he'd known she'd make him dance, he would have changed into something more suited to the exercise.

"Very good, lieutenant." Her cheekbones lifted as she beamed her satisfaction.

"I've bowed and walked two steps."

She pretended not to hear him. "And now we will join hands and walk two more to the front." She placed her cool hand into his and stepped forward onto her toes.

"I can't do that," Robert said, his mind on the smoothness of her skin rather than the dance. The gloves always worn at balls were conspicuously absent in their makeshift ballroom. Either she was too caught up in her teaching to notice, or she ignored the fact.

"Then take a normal step. If something is too difficult, walk normally with the music and all will be well."

They reversed the action, walking toward the back of their invisible set. These steps felt familiar, as though he'd danced them before.

"And if I can't use the correct foot for a step?"

"Use your left. It won't matter much if you're simplifying the steps anyway."

Robert raised an eyebrow. "You'll make me the laughing stock in fashionable society."

Miss Addison squared her shoulders. The candles' reflections flickered across the ringlets about her face, like the sun glittering on a lively sea.

"I think they will be impressed that through such a trial you have managed to find a way to live as normal a life as possible."

"You know they don't think that way," he said with a laugh.

"Perhaps they don't. But they should."

Robert didn't move. Neither did she. The firm set of her lips dared him to contradict her, but not in the harsh way he was used to getting from her. Nor did he hear pity in her tone. She believed what she said.

Miss Addison tore her gaze away and cleared her throat. "And now we circle around." She took his opposite hand and raised it above their heads. He knew the position. As she slid her hand around his waist, a thrill coursed up his side and set his heart racing. He put his hand on her slender waist and hoped the gesture didn't feel too eager.

They turned slowly, and for once he didn't hear the clunk of the wooden foot or feel the pain shooting up his leg. All that Trafalgar had taken from him, all the vibrance of life he craved, appeared before him in the form of a gray-eyed dancer whose smile he'd finally unlocked. He knew her pleasure came from his success, but he imagined, just for a moment, the curve of her lips meant something more.

When they finished their circle, she continued throwing out instructions for the rest of the dance with a flushed exuberance he'd never seen in her before. This wasn't the proud socialite he'd seen at the ball, but neither did he see the humiliated girl in the small Bristol house. Deep inside that pretty head, did there live someone he hadn't met?

They finished the dance, and Miss Addison clapped her hands together. "There, you see? You can dance, Lieutenant."

"Perhaps not in public, but—"

"But nothing. You danced, and you didn't think you ever could again." She bounced on her toes as she spoke. "Do you need to rest, or shall we try again?"

Yes, he very much wanted to try again.

Miss Addison hummed the tune, and Robert limped through the steps. It was terribly slow, and sometimes she hummed a little faster than he could keep up with, but she didn't seem bothered when she had to wait. The little heart he'd bought from the tin seller swung about her neck as they moved together. He hadn't anticipated the leap his own heart gave at the sight. It had seemed so plain a gift for someone as brilliant as Miss Addison. But now she wore it without shame.

They took each other by the waist again and began the circle. Robert's breath quickened, pulling in the scent of lavender that coiled through the still air of the parlor. He needed to take care, or he'd raise his hopes too high. Wearing the necklace was one thing. Accepting its giver another entirely.

Something knocked into the wooden foot, sending a jolt up his leg. Miss Addison cried out, letting go of him in a flutter of white skirts as she tripped over the blasted appendage. He whipped around trying to catch her, but the movement unbalanced him. His gut filled with the all-too-familiar rush of hurtling to the ground.

She hit the floor, and he twisted to avoid crushing her. The momentum sent him tumbling, his cursed foot thunking against the floor until he stopped against the legs of a sofa.

Miss Addison groaned, holding her head.

"Are you all right? I am so sorry." He started to push himself up, but her giggling halted him.

The giggle didn't stop, and for several moments she simply lay on the floor, hands draped over her stomach. She rolled to her side to face him.

He let his head drop back to the floor. His face must have been red as a marine's coat. "I'm sorry," he said again.

"I was going too fast. It wasn't you." Her laugh dissolved into a sigh. "I haven't had so interesting a dance in all my years in Society."

"Thank you, Miss Addison." Why did his heart ache at the lovely scene before him? Her hair fell back from her rosy face, and the soft fabric of her skirts fluttered against the floor. "You returned dancing to me."

But he couldn't believe she would restore everything he feared lost. No, he couldn't even think it.

Light footsteps on the stairs cut off Miss Addison's response. The clouds rushed into her eyes. She sat up rapidly and lurched to her feet. He didn't blame her. As much as he wished to bottle this moment and keep it forever, if someone caught them lying on the floor . . . Her reputation didn't need any more blemishes.

"Do you need help?" she asked.

He pushed up to his knees, waving her off, and used the sofa to get to his feet. How humiliating if he had to seek her help to right himself.

Miss Addison curtsied, the prim air returned to its place. "Thank you for the dance, Lieutenant."

And before he could ask her to stay, she ran from the parlor, taking with her the lavender magic that had infused the room. The cold swept into its place, spurred on by the distant rumbling from the retreating storm.

The name of the dance popped into his mind.

A Bristol Lass.

And he laughed to dispel the cold.

Holly slammed the door and secured the latch. She covered her mouth with her hand. What was she doing?

She raced to the desk and swept off the unfinished letter. A new piece of paper in place, she wrote the date and location, then "My dearest Miles." She needed to remember the feeling of flying about the room with Mr. Pelham. That was the world she wanted—the parties, the acquaintances, the fashion. Dancing with Mr. Pelham, she could bask in the gaze of every person in the room. She closed her eyes, trying to find the warmth of the radiance that came from being the envy of all. It had to be inside somewhere.

Mr. Pelham, and his darkly handsome features that could make any lady swoon. He knew just what to say, just what to do. In his dress, in his manner, he played the part of the perfect gentleman. How could she find fault in him? He had nothing lacking!

The pen drooped back to the desk. Her stomach churned as she stared at its ink-blackened tip, ready to write words of love to someone she should adore.

Mr. Pelham stirred up a giddiness Holly had lived for in Bath. She loved the stolen kisses and coy smiles. But could she really say she loved the man? She ran a finger along the white vane of the pen, not knowing how to answer the question. What did it mean to be in love, anyhow? She had seen plenty of fine marriages made from people who regarded each other as she and Mr. Pelham had.

Could there be more to it? Twirling about the parlor with the lieutenant sent sensations through her she had never felt before. She'd fought so hard to force down a smile while her traitorous heart kept time with the pounding rain. After falling to the floor, the pent-up electricity burst out in an uncontrollable laugh.

She hadn't felt radiant when dancing with Lieutenant Brenton.

She'd felt free.

And a piece of her soul she had so long repressed yearned for that liberation.

The tune of the flute agreed with her silent musings through the door. A hopeful melody this time. It coaxed forward a deep longing to feel that freedom again, until she wanted nothing more than to run back to the flute's master and into his arms.

Holly pushed away from the desk, hands pressed against her burning cheeks.

No. That wasn't her life now. Where would this silly infatuation lead? A simple friendship? More? The thought made her mouth run dry. She couldn't be content with so dull a life as he lived. What would happen after the euphoria of a wedding faded away? Her eyes squeezed shut. No, none of these ridiculous thoughts. She'd be left plastering cracks in the house alongside her poor husband.

Holly threw herself onto the bed and pulled the pillow over her head to block out the enchantment of the flute, which insisted she reconsider. The feathers stuffed inside the pillow cut off the melody, but they didn't get rid of the little tin pendant pressing into her heart.

Chapter Seven

Robert disliked using his cane, but it did help him cover more ground, which he needed today to clear his mind. The stony Miss Addison had returned by dinner last night. She hadn't even left her room that morning, asking for a breakfast tray instead of joining them at the table. He couldn't explain it. Father had once boasted of the good fortune of not having daughters, but now Robert sorely wished he had a sister for comparison. Surely all women weren't as temperamental as Miss Addison.

A light breeze blew up from the coast, bringing with it the fresh sea air. Robert couldn't see the water through the trees that edged the southern border of the property. It had been weeks since he felt the sway of the waves and the frigid spray against his face. He wouldn't have guessed he could miss it this much. Perhaps walking down to the beach would help set his head straight.

He changed course, heading for the little south path that ran past the stable and skirted around the sheep barn. He and his brother James escaped down to the beach nearly every day before James joined the navy. Robert couldn't remember how far it was, but it couldn't be more than a twenty minute walk.

As he passed the stable, Broom came out dragging a small, worn rowboat. "Sir, what would you like me to do with this?"

Robert hurried over as fast as the cane and wooden foot would let him. He knew that old boat. Flecks of blue paint speckled one side from his two eldest brothers' abandoned efforts one summer to make it a more worthy vessel. Gerald and Henry had rudely carved letters spelling out "The Maria"—their mother's name—across the back.

It wasn't the ship he craved, but it still made Robert grin. "Do you think it's still seaworthy?"

Broom shrugged, scrutinizing the inside. "I've seen better boats."

"Help me inspect it for holes."

He knew just what to do with *The Maria*. And though his heart beat a hopeless warning, he wasn't about to listen to it.

16 October 1807
Rowant Manor, Cornwall

My dearest Miles,

I have lived the coldest days of my life since leaving Bath. No light shines on this lonely corner where I find my aching soul. A piece of me is missing—the piece of my heart that was yours—and I cannot imagine ever finding myself whole without it.

Come for me, darling. Pull me from this abyss and let me show you the devotion you have called into doubt. Allow me to demonstrate to you how perfectly I can fulfill that role of wife and companion you seek. Let the world look upon us and see the bliss of two people so well suited for each other. We could be the envy of all, the image of marital harmony.

I beg you to think on the joy we will bring, not just to our families and acquaintances but to ourselves. Please tell me those dreams have not ceased for you in the weeks since last I saw your face. They have not faded for me, and I begin to doubt they ever will.

But some good has come from this awful separation. It has fixed in my heart the greatest truth I know—that I cannot live without you, and that no man could ever take your place in my heart.

All my love,
H. Addison

Chapter Eight

Robert glanced over his shoulder as he opened his former bedroom's door, hoping his stepmother did not wake at the click. He didn't know how heavily the woman slept, but just in case he blocked the light of his lantern as much as he could with his body so it couldn't creep under the door and give him away. His stepmother's room across the hall remained silent, to his relief. He could only imagine the shock on the poor lady's face if she saw him apparently sneaking into what was now Miss Addison's room.

Their previous meeting in this room had been shocking enough.

Normally he wouldn't dream of repeating such an encounter, but Miss Addison had an eye for the grand things of the world, and Rowant's grandest view would not wait for decent hours. He doubted even a young lady as elegant as Miss Addison could remain unaffected.

The door opened enough for him to slide the lantern inside. The young lady's deep breathing was the only sound within, uninterrupted from his earlier knock. She didn't flinch at the lantern's light. Something reflected back the light from the table beside her bed. He squinted and leaned forward.

The heart pendant.

"Miss Addison," he whispered through a smile. "Wake up."

She didn't stir.

He called her name again, a little louder. Her eyes blinked open, but the lids sank back down. Robert sighed. He didn't want to actually walk into her room again, but they'd have to move quickly to make it in time.

"Miss Addison?"

She sat up sharply, pulling the blankets up to her neck. "Lieutenant! What are you—"

Robert brought a finger to his lips, looking over his shoulder at his stepmother's room. Still no movement. "Get dressed and meet me downstairs. Bring your coat."

"What time is it?" Clearly she didn't realize the need for quiet.

"Four o' clock."

Her bleary eyes sharpened. "Who do you think I am, sir? A servant?"

In truth, most of the servants hadn't woken yet. "Just hurry."

She crossed her arms over the blanket. Little papers forming her perfect curls stuck out from odd angles around her head. "Some of us keep more fashionable hours than you do."

"Where we're going, there's no need to be fashionable."

Her eyebrows shot up. "Where are we going?"

He shook his head. Infuriating woman! If silence weren't his goal, he would have laughed. "To show you this decrepit house has some merit."

"Why must you show me at four o'clock in the morning? If you are attempting to change my mind, are you not afraid this dreadful hour will work against you?"

"What I have to show you will make up for it."

She harrumphed, more like the *Andersen*'s waspish bos'n than a svelte dancer from the ballrooms of Bath. "No more games. Tell me what you wish to show me, then I will make an informed decision."

With a chuckle, Robert retreated. "I'll tell you when we arrive. If you choose not to come, you'll never know what it is." And he clicked the door shut against the rest of her protests. Her grumbles filtered through the closed door, and the bed creaked. He'd piqued her interest, at least.

Robert moved down the stairs, wanting to go faster than his leg would allow. The excitement of this escapade overwhelmed the memories he knew would try to show themselves. He wouldn't let them win today, not like they had during the thunderstorm.

Today, on the second anniversary of the day his life changed forever, he would put Trafalgar behind him.

If only for a moment.

Holly sat with hands gripping the splintery sides of the feeble boat. It bobbed and dipped, and she had to bite her tongue to keep from squealing each time her stomach dropped. She didn't turn to watch the black shoreline receding as they ventured into the gray pre-dawn sea. Seeing it shrink away from them would do nothing to ease her nerves.

"Lieutenant, this is hardly proper," she said, trying to distract herself from the thought of all the water below them.

"Oh, come." Shadow concealed his expression, though they sat across from each other with knees nearly touching. A laugh tainted his voice. "We're practically cousins. There's nothing improper."

Holly pressed her lips together. "My father's half-sister marrying your father does not give us much of a relation." He took a breath as though to respond, but no words came.

"And replicating the impropriety of our first encounter here." She clucked her tongue. "I would not have expected it, even from you."

The lapping of the oars halted. He held up his hands, still grasping the wooden handles. "I stayed in the hallway. Propriety retained."

"Hardly."

The oars dipped back into the gentle waves, harmonizing with his low chuckle. She had to swallow back an unbidden laugh of her own, though she did not find the situation droll in the slightest. The lieutenant's company had a strange effect on her, driving her to actions she was not used to taking. Or inactions.

Nearly a week had passed since the last time they had been alone like this. An agonizing week. She'd sat down to write to Mr. Pelham a dozen times, but unlike the previous letter she didn't throw all her attempts in the fire. There weren't any. She had not made a single stroke on the page. It still sat empty on the desk, questioning her sudden lack of conviction.

If Mr. Pelham hadn't come by now, would he ever? She didn't think so. That path now seemed dark and distant as the shore. The disappointment did not hit with as much force as she anticipated, but it still hurt. She hoped in time, the thought of what might have been wouldn't sting so.

Lieutenant Brenton kept a steady rhythm with the oars. Though he faced away from their destination, he maintained a straight course toward the little island.

He looked nothing like the others she'd met in his predicament—large, old sea captains content to sit and wallow in misfortune. Though he had fooled her by his brooding attitude at the ball. Perhaps he didn't have so much strength as a normal man of the sea, but he had not let himself soften to life on land as Spencer had. No one would think Spencer a former officer on first meeting. No one could confuse Lieutenant Brenton for anything but a navy man.

Which was perhaps the only reason she had let him drag her into the ocean on a flimsy craft.

"Why are we going to an island at this obscene hour?" Holly asked, the fear returning. If this boat sank, that was the end of her. He wouldn't take her out if he didn't think it safe, would he?

"Come, Miss Addison, where is your taste for adventure?" The growing light illuminated his white shirt and cream-colored waistcoat and breeches. She could believe he had returned to the navy, if not for the exposed wooden foot. He had thrown his coat behind him in the boat and rolled up his sleeves despite the October chill. And he wore no hat, though she could hardly blame him without hypocrisy. In her haste, she'd forgotten her gloves. If Mama ever found out she'd gone out without gloves . . .

Holly snickered. Gloves would be the least of Mama's worries if she knew where Holly was at that moment.

"What is it?"

"Only that I have no taste for adventure, Lieutenant. I have a much stronger taste for elegant ballrooms and the comfort of friends."

Lieutenant Brenton didn't speak again until they reached the island. A crumbling lighthouse overgrown with foliage took up much of the rocky knob of land. Birds hummed from the bushes in anticipation of dawn. The lieutenant helped her from the boat, his hand warm around hers. He secured the boat, only stumbling over the false foot once. It was all Holly could do not to run to help him. She didn't want to wound his pride, and he righted himself quickly enough.

Finished, he turned and offered her his arm. "This way." She let him lead her around the island until they faced the eastern horizon.

"We're watching the sunrise?"

The lieutenant found a rock for her to sit on, then lowered himself to the ground beside it. "When was the last time you watched the sun rise, Miss Addison?"

"I'm not sure." Had she ever? It hadn't been since Bristol, if she had. She enjoyed sleeping until just before breakfast.

"This is the best spot to watch it. My brothers and I sneaked out to watch it sometimes when we were younger."

"Your mother let you?"

"She didn't know. At least, we don't think she did."

He went quiet, staring out at the waves. A few waterfowl paddled lazily about before them. Leaves rustled behind, and Holly felt caught in a wonderful daydream, one strangely devoid of gowns and society. Rays from the rising sun peeked over the dark streak of coastline on the other side of the cove, brushing the sky with orange and pink. It reflected on the gentle sea and in the green eyes that drew her attention more than anything around them.

"I offended you when we met at the ball," Lieutenant Brenton said.

Holly's shoulders slumped at the memory of her anger, when he'd intended a good-natured tease about their first meeting. "I shouldn't have been offended. You were only joking."

"Why did it offend you so much?"

Around them blacks faded to blues. Shadows fled. She studied him and the light playing in his hair, bringing back its youthful reddish hue from the little painting in her room. He looked hardly fit to walk among the gentry just now, with his careless attire. And yet she couldn't picture a man more worthy of the respect of his peers. He wouldn't judge her for this embarrassment kept deep in her heart.

Though he might laugh, and surprisingly she didn't mind.

"I try to forget my background," she said. "I don't like to be reminded."

Instead of laughing, he furrowed his brow. "Why is that?"

Holly's face grew hot, and she found it difficult to match his gaze. She turned back to the horizon. "I hated those years of poverty, bowing and scraping for any place in Society. I hated the whispers and condescending tones. Girls with half my skills in conversation or dance were paraded about town as the best of young ladies, while we shivered in a tiny house that was falling apart. None of our relations would speak to us." Her voice caught. "We were nothing."

The lieutenant sat forward, resting his arms on his knees.

"And when the estate passed from our relative to my father, I vowed I would not live another day as that frightened, humiliated girl." Holly straightened. "The world would see me as someone worth knowing. And they would love me." It sounded so ridiculous as she said it. Why had she told him all this?

"You aren't worried they will see you only as a dowry?"

Despite his kindly tone, the words cut. "I'd rather be seen as a dowry than a pauper." But the confident sentiment came out flat and uncertain. Was that how Mr. Pelham saw her? Just an addition to his fortune? A pretty face to adorn his figure, like a silk waistcoat or a new walking stick?

Lieutenant Brenton nodded slowly as he considered her words. She waited for condemnation. Or ridicule, as that was his usual mode of criticism. She deserved it, for all these silly fancies of that dandy.

"It is difficult when all you are known for is your misfortune," he said.

She lifted her head. No judgment marred his gaze. He knew better than she did what it meant to be known for misfortune. Her eyes followed his hand as it rubbed absently at the leather cuff holding the wooden foot onto the rest of his leg.

"Don't let your fear of what they think keep you from living, Miss Addison."

The sun's flaming burst broke through the last of the darkness. Flecks of gold floated on the waves as morning stretched into the sky.

Holly rested her hand lightly on his arm. "You would do well to listen to yourself, Lieutenant."

His lips twitched, then he let out a chuckle. His hand came up and hesitated above hers before resting atop it. It wasn't the breath-catching closeness she'd experienced in his arms that afternoon dancing in the parlor, and still the reassuring touch sent her head spinning. The glow of the morning seeped into her heart, chasing away any lurking thoughts of elegant society. And the memory of Mr. Pelham faded with the fleeing shadows.

Miss Addison didn't cling to the boat on the way back as she had on the journey there. She sat on the seat opposite him like a queen in command of the sea.

And though she may not command the waters, Robert knew she commanded his heart. He glanced behind him to check for hazards on their route back to shore and hoped she couldn't read his thoughts. Only when the heat cooled from his cheeks did he dare look at her again.

She'd gathered her hair back and tied it with a simple ribbon under her bonnet, which he found he preferred to Mrs. Phelps's more intricate styles. As much as he loved the memories of her dressed for the ball regularly weaving through his mind, the plain brown pelisse she wore this morning allowed her natural beauty to shine.

This Miss Addison had something he hadn't found in other young ladies. Few could even greet him without looks of pity or disgust. But to her, he was more than a cripple. More than a wooden foot. She wouldn't have gone through the effort to teach him to dance again if she only saw his wound and not the man attached to it. At least that was what he hoped.

"I think I like a leisurely boat ride in the morning," she said. "I only hope Mrs. Phelps and my aunt don't worry when we come in at noon."

Robert halted the oars. "Noon? It can't be later than half past seven." The pleasant tension of exertion ran up his arms from rowing.

"But we still have so far to go."

Robert looked back. Hardly. He'd get them there in twenty minutes.

"Next time I shall have to hire a faster boatman."

He narrowed his eyes as she primly stuck her nose in the air, but a grin lit her features.

"Are you insulting my speed, miss?" He gripped the handles of the oars.

"I shan't pay you a farthing for such a performance."

With a growl, Robert pulled back on the oars, doubling his speed. His arms quickly started to burn, but he kept the pace. Her eyes flashed with excitement, hair caught on the sea breeze.

"Half pay," she said, leaning forward.

He laughed at her goading and kept at his task, pushing the handles forward and then tugging them back faster. Soon he started panting. Sweat trickled down the side of his face. He wasn't used to such exercise, but the thrill pulsed through him.

"Lieutenant!"

Her warning cry didn't register until a violent jolt shot through the boat. A chilling crunch of wood on rock rent the day's calm. The floor of the boat pitched out from under their feet. Miss Addison screamed as the little craft dumped them head first into the water's cold embrace.

He fought against the waves trying to pull him down into their depths. Miss Addison! Where was she? He doubted she could swim. A numbness took hold of his chest, one he couldn't blame on the sea. He broke through the surface and twisted wildly about for a glimpse of her. He saw only foam.

Robert drew in air and dove back down, the brine stinging his eyes. He threw himself at a writhing form several lengths below the water. Precious air bubbles billowed from her as she tried to scream, eyes clenched tightly.

From behind he hooked one of his arms under both of hers and swam for the surface. She squirmed and kicked. The heel of her boot smashed into his leg where his stump met the wood. He nearly dropped her as pain seared up his leg. It took all his will to keep from gasping in the sea.

Keep going.

If he stopped, they'd drown. Gritting his teeth against the pain, he tightened his grip around her and beat his legs against the water. His lungs burned. Her nails clawed at his arm in her attempts to escape the deep.

Frigid air hit his face, and he sucked in its sweetness. Miss Addison coughed up water, sputtering and weeping. She thrashed, and he fought to hold her up.

"Miss Addison—Miss Addison, please—"

A heavy wave crashed into them, and she screeched until the sea cut off her air. Robert clasped her to him as it passed. The waves were increasing, pulling them too far from the capsized boat and rock, which the waters hid with each passing wave. They couldn't find safety there. He needed to get them to shore. Land hadn't looked this far away from the safety of the boat.

When the surge calmed, Miss Addison slashed at his arm. He tried to get her onto her back to float, but her thrashing pulled her downward.

"Miss Addison, stop!" He pulled her in tight, pressing her rigid back against his chest. "Holly, please!"

The flailing cut off, and she let out a whimper. Her ribs lifted and fell rapidly under his arm.

"Holly, I have you. You're safe."

When she'd stilled, he leaned back, keeping her close. He couldn't see her face, but her arms trembled as she clung to his.

Robert kicked his legs and pushed with his free arm. His pulse roared in his ears. With each stroke of his legs, the wooden foot pounded into his stump and the straps holding it loosened. Again and again the ache drove through him, and he and Holly sank a little lower.

Finally he could bear it no longer. He reached down and with stiff fingers grappled the buckle. Relief didn't flood through him like it usually did when he let the wooden leg fall. As the cursed thing drifted away, the pain only lessened a little.

He didn't pause to consider the loss. Rather, he kicked off the shoe from his good foot to help his progress and resumed his backward swim toward shore. Holly's skirts twisted around his legs as he pushed on, driven by her shaky breath. Despite the water's help to lift her, she felt heavy against him. Fire blasted through his limbs.

"We're going to make it," he whispered, more to himself than to her. "We're going to make it."

His strokes came slower and his breath rattled in his chest.

"We're going to make it."

His heel hit pebbles and sand. Robert murmured a prayer of thanks.

Holly cried out when he loosened his grip and again dug her fingernails into his arm, which stung from all her scratches.

"It's all right. You can stand."

She rolled off of him and stumbled as her feet hit the bottom. Her bonnet had fallen off when the boat turned over, and her yellow hair was plastered to her pale face.

Robert pushed himself on until his knees touched land. He crawled forward, arms quivering, and finally he cleared the water. He wheezed as he let himself drop to the sand. Holly's sobs filled his ears.

He didn't know how long he lay there. His body throbbed, especially what was left of his right leg. He couldn't remember feeling this drained of strength since his recovery from the amputation.

"Lieutenant?"

He didn't know where he found the energy to turn himself onto his back.

"Are you hurt?"

His face scrunched. How to answer that? He opened his eyes. She hovered over him, eyes wide and red from the saltwater.

He slowly sat up and met the sight of the distant rock. The upside down boat bumped contentedly against it. Nearby a little length of cherry wood rolled about in the waves.

"Your leg," Holly moaned. "How are we to get you home?" She raised her hands to brush away tears that lost themselves in the dampness of her face.

"You run ahead and send Broom back for me." Robert groaned and tried to stretch his hurting limbs. Sand stuck to the side of his face. He weakly brushed at it. "You need to change your wet clothes before you catch cold."

Her face pulled into a scowl. "You're as wet as I am."

"But I can't walk. I'll only slow you down."

He winked to soothe her worry, but instead of softening, her face hardened further. She rose to her feet, water squishing out of her dress and coat. Her hand extended toward him. He stared at it, then laughed.

"You can't carry me back to Rowant."

"I will not carry a lazy boatman such as you." He almost believed her irritation, except for the fear that still shone in her eyes. Her voice wavered through the confident front. "You are walking, sir, and I shall help."

Robert was too exhausted to protest. He let her help him stand. Her hand went around his waist, and she set his arm over her shoulders. When she turned her determined face toward him, he wanted so much to kiss it, from her creased brow to her firmly set lips. He didn't think a single woman from her fancy ballrooms would support a man back to the house. They'd still be blubbering on the sand calling for smelling salts.

"You don't have to do this." The head of the trail back to Rowant Manor lay so far down the beach, and hopping through sand would tire him much faster than solid ground.

"You didn't have to pull me from the water," she said, tightening her hold around him and nudging him forward.

He stayed still against her prodding, a smile pulling at the corner of his mouth despite his fatigue. "I would never have let you drown. One tries not to treat his . . . friends . . . that way." The sour taste on his tongue wasn't the ocean's brine. Friend? It felt so wrong to say. "Otherwise I would have left your brother to fend for himself. You Addisons have a knack for falling into the sea."

A grin almost cracked her stern facade. "We Addisons also do not allow our friends to sit around in wet clothes to catch cold." She attempted to pull him forward. Her arm around his waist was stronger than he expected from the lithe dancer, though it wasn't enough to move him. Still, he complied, and chuckled within at the flash of triumph on her face.

"We'll have to go slow," he said as they started off. He tried to keep as much weight off of her shoulders as he could, but his already weakened leg shook with the effort. If it hadn't been for the situation, he would have very much enjoyed walking with her tucked into his side like this.

She steadied him with her other hand against his waistcoat. "Save your breath. We have a long way to go."

Holly couldn't tell if sweat or ocean water now soaked her face. Her fondness for dancing and frequent opportunities to do so in Bath gave her the stamina to support Lieutenant Brenton across the beach. Part way up the path back to the manor, she'd exhausted the energy.

The lieutenant fared even worse. Tremors shook his body with each awkward step. He leaned more heavily on her the closer they got to the house. She tried to maneuver them around the rocks and pebbles littering the dirt path, but sometimes they were unavoidable. He winced as they hobbled over the rough ground.

"Let me sit," he finally said, not letting her push them further. His arm relaxed across the back of her shoulders, as though he meant to let go. "You continue on." Water dripped from his hair into his soaked shirt, his jacket having sank when the boat capsized. Clouds had stolen across the sky, bringing a chill with them. If he stayed behind, he'd surely catch cold. She would have offered him her coat, if it weren't sopping as well. Not that it would have covered much of him. His shoulder, perhaps.

"Broom cannot get a cart down here. You'll have to walk with him, just as you're walking with me now."

His rasping inhalations tore at her senses, and she fought to keep from wrapping him in her arms to steady him. She settled for grabbing his hand to keep his arm around her shoulders. This man had sacrificed so much to save her. He'd thrown away his wooden leg, his mobility and independence, to pull her from the sea's grasp. And all this time in Cornwall she had criticized his house, scorned his simple life. What men in Bath with two good legs could have saved her? Not many.

"Broom is stronger," he said. "He can—"

"You prefer Broom's assistance over mine?" She attempted a pout. Why was it so hard to make that face believable under Lieutenant Brenton's gaze?

He hesitated before he answered. His thumb traveled lightly over her knuckles, so soft she nearly mistook it for the breeze. "I cannot say I mind our current position."

Holly couldn't say she minded either, despite the harrowing experience they'd just survived and the wretched state of their clothes. Aunt Margaret would faint at the sight of them.

"Then let us keep going, if neither is in objection," Holly said. She nodded ahead. "We haven't far. See, there is the roof of the house."

"That is the barn," the lieutenant grumbled.

She nearly made a quip about how she couldn't tell the difference. But after all he'd done, how could she say something cruel about his home, even in jest?

He repositioned his arm around her and hopped forward. He didn't let go of her hand. She didn't wish him to.

When they finally reached Rowant's yard, the front door burst open. Aunt Margaret flew down the steps with a shriek. Holly's knees threatened to buckle in relief. She could only imagine how the lieutenant's felt.

"Gracious, where have you been? What happened?" her aunt cried. Her voice was louder than Holly had heard it since coming to visit. "Broom! Where's Broom? We need your help."

The young man appeared in the doorway, and Holly had never been so glad to see him. He ran to assist them up the stairs. Instead of them both getting Lieutenant Brenton into the house, Broom took Holly's place. Her aunt pulled her to the side to let the boy serve his employer. Holly leaned against Aunt Margaret. She had prayed so fervently for the end of their painstaking journey back to Rowant. She couldn't account for this silly disappointment.

Aunt Margaret pressed her for the story. She haltingly described their venture out to the island and subsequent crash. The terror she'd felt beneath the waves resurfaced in her telling. They'd come so close to drowning, thanks to her. She didn't know how he'd kept them afloat.

"Did anyone see you?" her aunt asked. "Oh, there will be rumors aplenty tomorrow. What are we to do? Your parents will be furious. They sent you here to get away from all that."

"Never mind rumors," Holly said. She hadn't seen anyone, not that she had looked. And she didn't care if someone had been there. "I am only grateful we are both alive. Come, Lieutenant Brenton needs help."

They took the stairs after the men, and those steps felt like a mountain to Holly's weary legs. They took the lieutenant into the parlor, his stepmother flitting about him and calling to servants.

Someone caught her sleeve as she made to enter the parlor, and she met Mrs. Phelps's pale face.

"Upstairs, miss. We need to get you warmed up."

Holly tried to pull away, but didn't have the strength. "I must see to the lieutenant."

"Mrs. Brenton and the lad will tend to him. You both need dry clothes."

Holly let the older woman drag her upstairs. They struggled to strip off the wet coat, gown, and underthings. She shivered in the cold air, her hair dribbling cold seawater down her back. Mrs. Phelps clicked her tongue and scolded as she helped Holly into a new chemise and wrapped her in a blanket. Then the woman bundled up her wet things and left to take them to the maid.

Holly shuffled to her trunk and pulled out short stays that laced up the front and a morning dress. Mrs. Phelps found her in the midst of pulling the dress over her head and rushed to help.

"Miss, oughtn't you get to bed? We need to warm you up so you don't fall ill."

"I must go to him." Bother, she had to flail as much as she had in the water to get into this dress. Mrs. Phelps set it right and helped her pin up the front.

"Whatever for? He's getting what he needs. I don't see what more you could do to help."

"I want to see him all the same." She *needed* to see him. The sight of his pain-shadowed face on their journey back would not leave her mind. She could still feel the tremors racking his body as he strained to keep moving. He wanted to get her back to the house, and she wouldn't leave him. Unbending as iron, the both of them.

Mrs. Phelps huffed. "At least let me braid up your hair. It'll need a good washing, for certain, but it seems you're in too much of a hurry for that."

Not only did the servant arrange her hair, she found stockings and house slippers and a shawl to drape about Holly's shoulders. Holly squirmed under the attention, itching to be downstairs with him. Usually she enjoyed dressing and paying mind to each detail. The lady's maid fussed with a fichu for added warmth. Concern wrinkled the corners of the older woman's eyes. Holly had seen it many times since coming to Cornwall but hadn't given the woman's worry much thought. When finally released from Mrs. Phelps's grasp, she squeezed the servant's hands.

"Thank you, Phelps."

Mrs. Phelps nodded, plump face brightening. "Go find your lieutenant, miss," she said as she shooed Holly away.

Holly didn't protest. She practically ran.

Downstairs the parlor was lit only by a fire in the hearth, as the curtains blocked the windows.

Someone had pushed a sofa up to it, and she could just see Lieutenant Brenton's head rested against the back. Fearing he slept, Holly crept around the side of the couch. The fire snapped, sending little showers of sparks into the air.

The lieutenant, a blanket cloaking his shoulders, watched the flames dancing through the wood. A little stool propped up his wounded leg. The other foot was wrapped in a bandage just visible under the hem of his trousers. She wondered how badly he'd injured it after the shoeless hike.

His finger rubbed a spot under his jaw, something he often did. The action pulled back his collar, which only loosely enclosed his neck without the cover of a cravat.

Her tongue felt thick in her mouth. "Are you well?" she managed.

His eyes flicked to her. One corner of his mouth curled upward. "Not you, too."

Holly didn't wait for him to invite her to sit. She lowered herself beside him on the sofa. He hadn't left much room, and her muslin skirt fluttered against his leg. "You don't want us to worry about you?" The fire's radiance warmed her face. At least, she thought it was the fire.

He shrugged a shoulder. "I'm injured, but I'm not an invalid." His voice was light as he said it, but she could see through the mask of his grin.

"Letting people care for you is not weakness, Lieutenant," Holly said.

He stared. Then blinked. "And . . ." His voice caught, and he dropped his gaze. "Do you—"

"Oh, Holly, I thought you'd stay in your room." Aunt Margaret whisked into the parlor with more blankets in her arms, and Holly scooted as far away as she could on the sofa. Her aunt didn't comment on how close she and the lieutenant sat. The maid following Aunt Margaret held a tray with two steaming bowls. "Cook was already making broth for tonight's soup. She didn't mind taking a little out for you." Her aunt held out a blanket, which Holly took and pulled around her, tucking in her skirts so they no longer lay against him. Then Aunt Margaret settled steaming bowls into their hands.

"Is there anything you need?" she asked her stepson. He shook his head. "I'll find Broom to stoke the fire. Mary, take this tray back to Cook and have her boil water for tea." Her aunt rushed out of the room. "I'll return in a moment."

Holly sipped at the broth, savoring the herby richness that filled her belly and warmed her from within. It soothed the rawness of her throat from swallowing saltwater. When she'd finished, she set her bowl on a side table and took the lieutenant's from him. Then she turned toward him, pulling the blanket up to her face.

"Thank you," he said softly. "For earlier."

Her eyebrow shot up. "For panicking like a ninny and almost making us drown? You are most welcome, sir."

He chuckled. "That isn't what I meant."

"For goading you to row faster, then? And crashing us into a rock?" She leaned her head back against the sofa like his.

"Oh, I just thought you fancied a little sea bathing."

Holly's jaw dropped, and his eyes flashed with glee. "I beg your pardon, sir! I would never ask a gentleman to assist me in sea bathing."

"Better a handsome young man than the shriveled old women who usually do the job."

Holly shook her head, trying to look stern and failing miserably.

"Mostly I wanted to thank you for helping a broken man who couldn't even walk back to his own house." The mirth fled his eyes, replaced by something Holly couldn't quite name. But it made her melt inside, like metal thrown into the fire.

Heart fluttering wildly, she reached up and caught his face between her hands. Her fingers smoothed over his jaw, sending all sorts of wonderful sensations scampering down her arms.

"You are not a broken man, Robert," she whispered. "I prefer you just the way you are, no matter what you think you are missing."

She snatched her hands back and buried them under the blanket. If her face hadn't reddened before, she knew it must be scarlet now. Of all the unguarded things to do! She ducked her head and let it rest against his shoulder to hide her embarrassment. His shoulder moved with every sharp breath he took. His breathing nearly matched the speed of hers.

Her blanket moved, and a moment later his fingers wrapped around hers. He slipped her hand back to his face, pressing his cheek into her palm.

Holly looked up into his brilliant eyes, her face so close she could feel his warmth on her lips. He still had the scent of the sea on his skin. The fire crackled, but nothing else stirred around them. And if someone asked her just then what she wanted most in the whole world, she knew what she would have said.

Her eyes strayed to his lips, and he tilted his face toward her. "Holly, I . . ."

How had she ignored all of this? Him, her feelings, life itself. She'd hidden them all behind her desire to return to Society. Now they pulled her in, to him and the world he offered, and though the silk-stockinged lady in her mind screamed protests, her heart had no wish to change course. If dancing in his arms felt so wonderfully different from anything else, she couldn't believe his kiss any less captivating. Her eyelids fell. She leaned in. If she'd swallowed the fire before them, she didn't think she could feel any warmer.

The sound of a clearing throat made Holly bolt to her feet, the blanket dropping to the floor. Broom stood at the doorway, wide-eyed gaze sweeping from her to Robert and back again. For once he didn't wear his scowl.

"Miss—Miss Addison, there's a gentleman here to see you." A figure moved in the hall behind him.

Her stomach sank, as though the boat had tossed her into the sea once again. "Who is it?" She knew. Who else could it have been?

The gentleman brushed past Broom and presented himself with a flourish.

"No need to worry that pretty head anymore, darling. I've come to take you home."

Holly stood immobile by the sofa.

Mr. Pelham.

Chapter Nine

Robert stiffened, craning his neck to see who had entered the room. Holly's pale face should have confirmed it. Near the door, the dandy he'd seen her hanging onto at the ball held out his hand. The man wore a deep red coat and boots that shone even in the dim light of the sitting room.

"Your parents wish us to return as quickly as possible. They cannot bear another moment without you." Mr. Pelham seized Holly's hands and drew her in. "Nor can I."

Robert's blood ran cold as the gentleman lifted Holly's hand to his lips and wrapped each knuckle in a kiss. He wanted to sink back into the sofa, but he couldn't look away.

"My parents sent for me?" Holly blinked. Some of the paleness lifted from her cheeks.

"Of course, darling. This wasn't meant to be a permanent separation."

What was he talking about? He'd cut off their engagement and accused her of disloyalty. The scoundrel had dragged her reputation through the muddy streets of Bath. What right did this man have to sweep in here and carry her away after casting her off?

"Call for your servant. Have her pack your things. We leave as soon as you can be ready."

A spark in Holly's eyes silenced the objection Robert itched to voice. If it was what she wanted, could Robert argue? What was Rowant to the Pelham estate? Nothing to her. A decrepit house that reminded her of a past she wished to erase.

"With good roads and a little haste, we'll arrive in time to accompany our families to the theatre." Mr. Pelham winked at her, earning a faint laugh.

Robert finally let himself fall back into the sofa, his arm dropping limp across the place Holly had sat. So it was over. He'd been a fool to let himself think that dream would happen. Life had set her in his path, taunted him with the idea that someone might be convinced to see past the crippled leg. Holly had only looked at him as a last chance when her life lay in shambles. For a moment he'd let himself believe. The fire that had pulsed through him just a moment before shriveled to ash.

"Yes, of course," she said. "I'll send for Phelps. Oh, but I have a gown and pelisse in shambles. They need washing and mending." Holly's hand shot to her frizzed hair. "I am hardly presentable. Perhaps we should wait to leave until tomorrow." Her eyes darted to Robert. Was that sympathy or worry in their depths? He looked away quickly, not wanting to see either.

"Leave the gown. Your mother has employed an army of mantua makers, and I daresay you will not have a minute to spare between fittings."

"That's a little extreme for a welcoming gift," Holly said. But Robert could hear her tentative pleasure.

"Oh, but it isn't a welcoming gift." Mr. Pelham's voice lowered, taking on an almost gentle tone. Almost. "We've restructured our agreement. The vicar will read the bans on Sunday."

"The . . . bans?" she echoed softly, taking a step back.

This Sunday. Robert clenched his eyes shut. Why had he allowed himself this silly fantasy? If he had his wooden foot, he would have stood and charged from the drawing room to escape this private conversation. Now the leg bobbed in the ocean, another testament to his stupid judgment.

"My darling Miss Addison, won't you forgive me?" The dandy grabbed for her hand and dragged her toward him again. "When I read your letters, I saw the error of my actions. I couldn't stay away."

Those blasted letters. She was begging Pelham to return. Robert should have known.

"I . . . Have you made the acquaintance of Lieutenant Brenton? He has been a most accommodating host."

What was she doing? Her anxious eyes met his, but he didn't hold them for long.

Mr. Pelham moved stiffly around the sofa to shake his hand, then balked at the sight of his missing leg. "Ah, yes. Lieutenant." He pulled his hand back and settled for a bow. Skepticism flared across his face. "What is your relation, might I ask?"

Robert bristled. "I am her cousin," he growled.

Distrust vanished from the dandy's face. Robert ground his teeth. "A relative. Very good. The kingdom is indebted to you for your service, sir."

Hollow words, accentuated as Mr. Pelham turned his back and forgot his debt in the joyous raptures of engagement. "Come, let us fetch Phelps," he said. "I don't wish to stay in this forsaken county one minute longer than is needed. When we get to Bath, everything will be right again."

"Yes. Right again." Robert almost couldn't hear her.

"Come, we haven't a moment to lose, darling," Pelham snapped.

"Then I will say my goodbyes." She paused, and Robert's breath stopped with her. "Lieutenant?"

He didn't turn around.

She left the word hanging, syphoning the air from the room without any more words to follow. Was that pity he heard in her strained tone? She needn't bother with apologies. He'd heard enough of them.

The dandy began to grumble about the hour once more. Their footsteps retreated down the hall, leaving Robert alone with the popping fire. As he watched, the topmost log crashed forward. A cloud of cinders billowed up around it before settling back into the hearth. He wasn't close enough to catch their sting against his skin, but he felt them, as though he'd drawn them in to swirl inside, singeing every sore piece of his heart as they danced.

Robert had one consolation. He didn't feel the throbbing pain in his leg anymore.

Mrs. Phelps finished tying up the last curl in its paper. "There, that must feel better."

Holly wished it did. She hadn't had a proper bath—the inn didn't provide for that—but they'd washed her hair in a bowl of steaming water and wiped the dried saltwater from her skin as best they could. In no time, all evidence of her time in Cornwall was cleaned away.

And it left her more empty than she would ever have guessed.

"I'll take this out and come back with some tea," Mrs. Phelps said, lifting the bowl and heading for the door. "Just rest yourself, miss."

The door shut, and Holly trudged from the little parlor into the bedroom. She pulled on her dressing gown over her shift and sighed. Her gaze fell on the open trunk. Sitting on top of her clothes, the little tin heart shone in the faint light from the parlor hearth. It must have fallen from her dressing gown pocket when she removed it from the chest. Holly scooped the pendant up to admire its perfectly polished surface, then clasped the necklace around her neck. Its weight against her chest brought a little of that peace she missed since walking out of Rowant's front door.

The tranquility deserted her at the memory of Robert's—Lieutenant Brenton's—hollow stare when Mr. Pelham entered the room. Somehow she'd caused it, the lifelessness in those usually vibrant eyes. Her arms wound around her stomach in an attempt to still the rolling within. One moment she'd melted under the alluring fire of his gaze, and then that gaze had turned to unfeeling steel. So unnerved by the change, so worried she would let her opportunity with Mr. Pelham go for fear of what Lieutenant Brenton thought, she'd fled the parlor without so much as a goodbye. How could she have done that to him, after all he'd endured?

But this was what she wanted. She wanted to be Mrs. Miles Pelham and prance through town on his arm, dressed in the finest money could buy. The parties they would host, the acquaintances they would make, the elegance of the life they would live . . . she couldn't give that up for a fourth son with no doubt less than a thousand per annum.

Holly drifted back toward the fire, hoping to dispel the chill that filled her. She willed Mrs. Phelps to return quickly with the tea. Her fingers caught hold of the heart pendant as she took her previous seat. The logs before her rustled in the flames. For an instant, she sat on the sofa in Rowant Manor's parlor, the lieutenant's breath on her lips. Her hands covered her face and she turned away from the hearth.

She hadn't struggled with thoughts of Mr. Pelham this way, unable to clear him from her mind and yet not wanting to. Her hand came up to her forehead. She thought she loved Mr. Pelham, but the remorse had never hit her heart this sharply at the thought of never having him. Holly took a shaky breath. She'd made her choice, the choice her family wished. The choice *she* wished.

Hadn't she?

Holly stood at a knock on the door. Mrs. Phelps at last. But a ruby tailcoat sailed into the room, and with it the beaming face of Mr. Pelham. She clutched her dressing gown more tightly around her. With her hair up in papers, she must look a sight.

"What do you mean by this, sir?" She forced the corners of her mouth upward, hoping she looked eager enough.

"I had to see you one last time before I retired for the night." He cut the distance between them and snatched her into his arms. Holly couldn't help the rigidity that ran up her spine.

His eyes fell on the necklace. "What is that you're wearing?"

Holly's hand went back to the heart pendant. "Only a trinket I found in Cornwall."

"No need to wear such plain things now." His lips twitched. "Or associate with such low company."

"I found I did not mind it so much."

Her response sent a shadow across his face. But he quickly remedied it with a brilliant smile. "Only a few more weeks until you're mine, darling," he said, and pushed his lips against hers.

For the first time since announcing their engagement, the silly excitement that usually greeted such a gesture fell silent. She stood, allowing him his fill. Her throat constricted against the fierceness of his kiss.

He pulled away slowly. "What is it?"

Holly took a step back, but his arms didn't release her. A jittery panic ran through her veins. She pushed against his chest, but still his arms wouldn't budge.

"Do you think we should have the bans read this early? We've been apart for so long, surely it makes better sense to wait." She fought a tremor that tried to find its way into her voice.

"We'll have two weeks. That's long enough." His eyebrows dropped low over his eyes. "What is this about?"

Holly pushed harder. "Only that I wish to have a little more time for preparations. To make certain this is the right decision."

His arms finally loosened. "Right decision? Why wouldn't this be the right decision?"

Holly swallowed and clutched the hems of her sleeves.

"You seemed to think it right when you posted letter after letter begging me to come for you."

Her eyes squeezed shut. "Yes, I did."

"Do you know what my character will suffer in the eyes of our friends when they hear I've gone after the woman who wronged me? Truth or not, that is what Society sees. I am returning to you all we once had." His voice lowered dangerously. "Did Cornwall change you so much to make you reconsider?"

"I haven't reconsidered. I am very grateful." The words she spoke stabbed at her uncertainty. She didn't feel gratitude just then. She didn't even feel guilt for its absence.

"Is this about the sailor?" he growled.

"Why would you think—" Holly shrieked as he grabbed the little tin heart and yanked. The chain dug into the back of her neck before it broke. Her hand flew up to touch the tender ridge the necklace made.

Mr. Pelham held the pendant up, sneering as it swung from his fingers.

"If you think you cannot trust me, we can cancel the engagement again," she cried, then clapped her hands over her mouth. What was she saying?

"You've made your decision. The contracts have been signed."

He flung his arm toward the hearth. A little silver flash tumbled through the air, the chain writhing behind it, and lost itself in the hissing fingers of fire.

"No!" Holly lunged for it, but Mr. Pelham snatched her arm.

"You will have all the jewels you want once we are married. Better than that horribly plain thing."

He released her and left the room without looking back.

Holly snapped up the poker. The necklace had fallen onto the stone just below the andirons. With trembling hands, she looped the end of the poker around the chain. Tiny droplets of starlight trailed behind the pendant as she pulled it out, a sob ripping from her throat. The drips left behind glimmered in the soot.

The chain melted just below the iron, leaving a silver stripe across the poker and dumping the little heart onto the brick around the hearth. She released the poker and dropped to her knees. The pendant steamed and popped. Now the point of the heart skewed to the left, and bubbles marred the once mirror-like surface.

Holly didn't know the door had opened until Mrs. Phelps's cry of alarm. She pulled a towel off the table and scooped up the scalding trinket before the servant helped her to her feet. Mrs. Phelps fussed over the dressing gown, but Holly couldn't pull her eyes from the ruined heart in her hands.

What had she done?

Chapter Ten

Robert tried to focus on the notes flowing through the flageolet. For so many hours he'd practiced stilling his worries and sorrows in the tunes the Irishman had taught. His fingers moved over the instrument's holes without thought. Most days the melodies helped calm his soul when images of war and memories of pain overwhelmed him.

Once in a while, it didn't work, and tonight was one of those nights.

Despite that day marking the anniversary of Trafalgar, it wasn't remembrances of that fateful battle which refused to let him be. Sawdust and gunpowder didn't cloud around him, nor did ear-splitting bursts rain down deadly splinters.

Robert let the flute drop to his lap. Moonlight pooled on the floor of his old bedroom. Intoxicating lavender hung in the air, suffocating him. Memories of his mother and Holly wove themselves together in his mind. Two women he could never have again. He'd made himself used to the thought of never seeing his mother again, but Holly . . .

He slid his fingers under the sleeve of his opposite arm. Crescent-shaped scabs dotted the skin where Holly had dug in her nails after the boat overturned that morning. They would soon fade, but Robert knew with a certainty that the memories never would.

Holly clung to the wall of the coach as they passed into Bath. Mrs. Phelps had fallen asleep long before, and Mr. Pelham tried to take advantage of the privacy. A month ago she would have obliged a stolen kiss. Today she leaned away and pressed her face against the window.

He scowled from the opposite side of the carriage, and she pretended not to notice. She'd seen less of his smiles and more of his disgruntlement since they left Rowant. Her fingers traced her pocketbook, where she'd tucked away the mangled heart pendant. Mr. Pelham was simply out of sorts from the fatigue of traveling so far in such a short time. That explained his outburst and these scathing looks. Some rest would return him to his usual dashing self, and they could refocus their efforts on the impending marriage.

The coach passed a pair of boys sailing paper boats in the gutter. The boys laughed as their boats flopped this way and that. Her brother used to sail boats like that, back before fortune and Society demanded decorum. The happy sounds faded into the distance as they made their way toward her family's spacious townhouse.

Perhaps she could convince the family to retire to Nettleton Place, her father's house in the country, for the winter. It was closer to London than Bath, wasn't it? There they could help her younger sister, Sarah, prepare for her first Season. She didn't think her parents would mind if they pushed the wedding back to the end of the Season, so as not to outshine Sarah.

What was she thinking? Of course they would mind. They couldn't parade their conquest of the Pelham wealth if she married at the end of the Season and Society was in the midst of fleeing town.

A rat pulled itself out of the gutter, watching the coach with beady eyes. Holly shivered and turned away from the window.

No, it was better to follow through with the marriage plan. Once the deed was done, she couldn't chase silly ideas of living in a crumbling manor in the middle of Cornwall with . . . Holly swallowed. In a short time she would forget the last month, with all its strange feelings. She would have all she ever desired. All she needed. And in years to come she would thank herself for not falling prey to romantic notions.

The carriage stopped, and Holly threw herself into her mother's waiting arms. She couldn't explain the tears that rushed forth, and for the first time in years her mother didn't try to cover the unsightly display. Her arms tightened around Holly, but they couldn't pull together all the broken pieces.

Robert rested against the bank of earth, cane dropped unceremoniously at his side. He closed his eyes, letting the chill sea breeze wash over his sweat-streaked face. It tugged at his hair, a sensation so familiar it almost brought a smile, and ruffled the papers in his hand. His limbs rested limp against the sand after the exertion of walking from the house to the shore without the wooden foot. It was a good sort of ache.

He wanted to loosen his fingers and let the wind tear the sheets of paper away. For months, he'd known they were coming. Heavens, he'd requested them. But he didn't expect their arrival to hurt this much. Perhaps if he hadn't lost all hope with Holly's departure two weeks ago, receiving this letter would have been easier to bear.

"Mrs. Brenton sent me with this."

Robert cracked one eye open, glowering up at Broom. The lad held what looked like an enlarged chicken leg—a wooden stick attached to a leather cone with straps dangling from the end.

He shut the eye again. "I am not wearing that."

"You'll walk better with it, sir."

"I don't want it."

"She wondered why and said to stop acting like a sulking child."

Robert sat up. "Margaret said that?" With as shy as that woman was, he couldn't imagine her saying something so critical.

Broom shrugged. "I might have added that last bit." He dropped to the sand, crossing his legs before him. "Why don't you like the peg leg?"

Robert leaned back again, too worn to scold the young man. He pulled his hat down over his eyes. "With the wooden foot, I could at least pretend I wasn't broken."

From the darkness under his hat, he only heard waves crashing against the sand.

Someday the emptiness would get easier. He'd hoped nearly two weeks would put the disappointment behind him.

"You could get a new one made," Broom suggested.

"When? I have no plans to travel to London."

"There's no one closer who makes them?"

There was. In Bath. And he wasn't going there anytime soon.

A gull called from somewhere nearby. Perhaps if he pretended to sleep, Broom would go away. Not that he didn't like the lad.

"The way I see it, there's only two solutions, sir."

The peg leg or the cane. Yes, he knew. And he'd already decided which to use. It wasn't as if he were going out in Society any time soon. Society in the area was sparse, and they'd had few visitors since arriving. His stepmother turned down enough invitations to dissuade the few prominent farmers from seeking better acquaintance.

"Either you forget the lady, or you marry her yourself."

Robert sat up so quickly his hat fell to the sand. "That is not your place, lad. Nor is it Mrs. Brenton's."

Broom nodded, his tumultuous hair bouncing. "Only saying what I see."

What sort of advice was that, from a boy not even ready for marriage? What did he know?

"Can I help you back to the house, Lieutenant?"

Robert shook his head. "I am not a lieutenant any longer." He waved the papers in his hand. "My official letter of discharge. I am now nothing more than a humble country gentleman." And a sulking, disfigured one at that.

"Yes, sir." Unprompted, Broom got to his feet and disappeared back up the path without another word.

Robert plucked up a length of seaweed and rolled the slimy strip through his fingers. Holly wanted the life Mr. Pelham could give her. He wouldn't deny her that, if she wanted it so badly. Robert couldn't give her a glamorous existence. Only a steadfast love and a laugh through the dark times. Even if he didn't always feel like laughing.

His eyes strayed over to the spot where he and Holly had emerged from the sea. She'd been frozen with fright, and still she worried over him.

I won't carry a lazy boatman such as you. You are walking, sir, and I shall help.

The grin pulled at his lips. Her gray eyes had flashed with so much determination. That sort of woman could survive life in a little manor. She could even make the best of it. How would it be to have a woman such as that by his side?

It would never be, his heart whispered. She belonged to another man.

Robert glanced at the peg leg, which Broom had left in the sand. Before he could think too hard, he seized it and shook it clean. He rolled up the leg of his trousers to expose the mangled knob left from Trafalgar's operation. He didn't stop to examine its scars and bemoan his fate.

After shoving his leg into the leather holster, he pulled the straps tight and secured the buckle. He used the cane to stand. Once he cleared the sand, he made a faster pace toward Rowant Manor. As much as he hated the appearance of the peg leg, he'd forgotten how much easier it was to move with it. In the Mediterranean there hadn't been an option of a well-made foot, and he'd made himself proficient on the odd-looking peg. He sailed over the rough ground compared to his tedious march with Holly. Though he wanted to stop and savor the images of her resolved face that filled his mind, he kept his pace. There was no time.

Robert couldn't say what he'd do once he made it to the house. Send Broom to collect his things. Yes, that was where to start. His stepmother would worry, but that couldn't be helped. Why had he sat here wallowing in his grief, when there was still a chance to change their fates?

Chapter Eleven

Robert sat in the Bath shop listening to the jolly owner prattling on to his assistant as he measured and tested different styles of feet. He'd have to pay handsomely for this replacement, but it wasn't the sum that made his stomach churn.

Tomorrow Holly would wed Mr. Pelham unless he put a stop to it, and Robert's confidence had failed him. On his way to the shop, he'd nearly stopped by the townhouse to leave his card. If she saw it and still cared, she would contact him, wouldn't she? But what if she didn't see it in time? How would he know if she shunned him or missed the card? Time ticked away.

Robert wore his lieutenant's coat, his other day coat having sunk with *The Maria*. He hadn't even thought to bring his dress coat, a stupid oversight. What her family would think of him, he didn't want to know.

"Weddings all about these days," the assistant said, fitting another false foot to Robert's leg. Not tall enough. He suppressed a groan. He'd hoped to have something besides the peg when he presented himself to the Addisons. "Strange for November."

The shopkeeper chuckled as he noted measurements in a ledger. "Saw Jacob's employer Mr. Pelham in the street yesterday. That man does not have his head on right." He wagged the pen at his assistant. "A mess, that one."

Robert stiffened.

"Is he marrying Lord Goswell's daughter tomorrow?" the assistant asked.

Lord Goswell? Robert stayed still, trying to keep his face impassive.

The shopkeeper shook his head gravely. "The Addison girl."

"After he dropped the engagement with her? And all the rumors about courting the Goswell lady?"

The older man sighed. "Despicable man, that one." His eyes shot to Robert. "Not an acquaintance of yours, I hope?"

Robert shook his head. Goswell? The man had been courting an earl's daughter since her parents sent Holly away? He shifted in the uncomfortable chair. The assistant began unbuckling the leg.

The shopkeeper lowered his voice. "Jacob says Pelham is after a dowry to cover debts. Courted Lord Goswell's daughter for months, then thought he'd have an easier go at Miss Addison and caught her before he realized he'd done it. The Pelhams aren't ones to argue with Society, and Society thought the engagement was settled, so Mr. Pelham made it so.

He later decided Miss Addison's dowry wasn't enough, but when the earl whisked his daughter away, Pelham figured any dowry was better than no dowry. Wrapped up the whole business, pretty as you please. The scoundrel will get away with it, and the Addisons will be none the wiser."

Robert snatched up his peg leg and fastened it with shaking hands.

"I think I can have this ready by next week, sir."

He nodded his head in thanks toward the man and assistant and fled into the street. Hang his blasted peg leg, and hang Mr. Pelham. He should have taken the chance to see Holly that afternoon. Shops all about him were closing their doors for the night. Street lamps were being lit. No doubt the Addisons would soon sit down to dinner.

He'd interrupt like a classless buffoon. But he couldn't let Holly marry the cad.

He set off toward the Addison residence, praying his leg would hold up that long. Peg leg or no, this was his last chance.

Holly was drowning.

The stifling heat of richly dressed bodies crammed into the dining room made her want to gag. The fish on her plate lay untouched, the wine in her glass undisturbed. What she wouldn't give for a wind off the sea to clear this all away.

"Holly, are you well?" Spencer whispered from the seat next to her. Their mother's tittering at Mr. Pelham's latest joke covered the sound. Holly pretended she didn't hear him. She didn't know how to answer.

"How good it will be to finally see the two of you settled," Mr. Pelham's mother said farther down the table. "I don't know why we thought to wait until February before. You can make all your visits through Christmas, and then you shall be ready with all the new acquaintances for the Season."

"Let us host a ball, Mother, as soon as there are friends enough in Town," Mr. Pelham said. "And any who have not found their way to London yet shall regret their tardiness."

A ball. Heavens, no, she didn't want to think about a ball. Balls only reminded her of the last one and seeing the lonely lieutenant who sequestered himself in the corner. Her face flushed. No, she couldn't think of him. But the memory wouldn't fade.

"Ah, look. The blushing bride." Mrs. Pelham sighed. "What a handsome pair you will be tomorrow morning. What a lucky man you are, Miles."

Holly's stomach twisted. How could the wedding be tomorrow?

Her mother beamed at the praise. "Oh, but it is we who are lucky. What a fine family Holly will join us to."

Mrs. Pelham smiled into her glass, which was now mostly empty after several refillings. "You are most kind, madam."

Holly's younger sisters said little, taking in the pomp and excitement of the evening. Their closest friends and family could speak of nothing else but the looming wedding. Holly knew she shouldn't expect anything less. She knew she should welcome it, for she'd never have this attention again.

The Holly Addison from two months ago would have been horrified at this new Holly, longing for Rowant's cozy dining room, with Aunt Margaret quietly focused on her food and Lieutenant Brenton throwing her smiles and winks from the other end of the table. The food, in all its simplicity, had been more palatable than what she now had before her.

Mr. Pelham raised his glass. "A toast!" All glasses at the table lifted. Holly nearly tipped hers over as she grasped it with a quivering hand. When all had followed his lead, he said, "To the future Mrs. Miles Pelham, and the union of these two fine families. May we ever have an excess of friends and a deficit of worries."

"To Mrs. Pelham!"

Holly set down her glass without taking a sip. She couldn't do it. She wanted to run from the room, to call off this insanity. But she'd brought this on. She had been the one to write to Mr. Pelham, begging him to remember his adoration, begging him to come for her. Her body stayed glued to the chair.

The misshapen heart hidden in her bodice pressed into her chest. A new chain about her neck allowed for better discretion, but Mr. Pelham still eyed it each time she wore it, even if he couldn't see the pendant.

A footman stole into the dining room and spoke to the butler. The older man glanced at the family, then gave the footman a sharp shake of his head. The footman persisted, and the butler finally waved him off. He made his way to Holly's father. She leaned in to hear.

"A Mr. Robert Brenton, sir. He requests . . ." The butler glanced at the Pelhams. "He requests a private audience with Miss Addison."

Holly's heart stopped. Her hand flew to the pendant.

Mr. Addison huffed. "Now?" he asked, a bit too loudly. "Why did you not send him away? Does he not know we have a wedding in the morning?"

"The footman said he insisted it could not wait, sir. He wishes to speak to her tonight."

He came. For her. After all she'd done.

"Who is at the door?" Mr. Pelham asked, breaking from a conversation with his mother. Holly hastily looked away.

Spencer started to rise. "I—I'm sorry, Father. The footman must be mistaken, I am sure he meant me. I saw the lieutenant at the pump room and invited him for tea. I wasn't thinking."

Holly's shoulders slumped. Of course he would come for Spencer, and at dinner, so she couldn't see him without an awkward exit. No one, not even her parents, knew that she'd stayed at his house while in Cornwall. They assumed Aunt Margaret stayed at Rowant alone. Mr. Pelham had kept his silence, whether out of anger or jealousy, she did not know. But she couldn't leave her future husband and mother-in-law to meet her brother's friend without causing more of a scene.

Their mother grasped Spencer's arm, preventing him from leaving, and glared. "You didn't go to the pump room today. You haven't been in nearly a week."

Spencer flushed. "It must have been last week, and the date slipped my mind."

Mr. Pelham glanced from Holly to her brother, then to her mother. "Who is it?"

"What shall I tell him, sir?" the butler asked, face reddening as all turned their attention to the disruption.

"Send him away."

Away. Where would he go? Back to Cornwall, and out of her life forever, leaving her to be the empty-headed Mrs. Miles Pelham in her elegant cage.

"No!" Holly stood, the action pushing her plate and toppling her glass. A dark stain crept across the cloth between her and Mr. Pelham on the other side of the table. "Please send him in." If only for a minute.

Her parents turned horrified faces toward her as the butler scrambled out of the room. She didn't meet their eyes, or the eyes of anyone else in the room. She stared at the door.

Her mother reached across Spencer and yanked at her hand. "Sit down, for heaven's sake, Holly. Why do you care about seeing an old acquaintance of your brother's? You don't even know him."

Robert limped in, his lost wooden foot replaced by a peg. He stopped inside the door and faced her friends and kin. Muttering rippled through the room at the sight of his disheveled hair and rumpled lieutenant's coat.

Her chest swelled as she breathed for the first time in weeks, gasping in the sweet air she'd so desperately craved. "Robert, how good to see you." She cringed at the pleasantry's flat taste on her tongue. Whispers twirled through the room at her informal address.

Robert's resulting grin tore at her heart. She didn't deserve his smiles.

Mr. Pelham pounded the table, upsetting another glass. "What is the meaning of this? What are you doing here?"

"Explain, Holly," her father said through clenched teeth.

Her hands twisted together. She had the attention of every person in the room. What a foolish girl she had been. That afternoon by the fire, she knew what she wanted. It had appeared in her mind, clear as the Cornish sky on a bright day. She let Mr. Pelham's unexpected appearance bring back the trifling fancies of the past.

Spencer tried to ease the tension with a greeting of his own, but Robert didn't spare him a glance. Something shone in his eyes as he fixed them on her. Hope? The ends of his lips curled hesitantly.

Holly placed her hands on the table, to steady herself as much as to appear in control. "If Mr. Pelham may change his mind about our engagement, I feel I have the right to do so as well." She flinched at her mother's shriek. Mrs. Pelham's jaw nearly fell to her lap.

Mr. Pelham formed his hands into fists. He took a step toward her, and she was grateful for the table between them. "You would choose a peg-legged sailor over my wealth and station?"

Holly met his wild snarl with an even gaze, despite the instinct to shrink away. "Yes."

An array of horror and rage flashed over the faces of the group. Only Spencer's eyes sparkled. Holly pushed out her chair and used all her self-command to glide around the table toward him, when really she wanted to fly.

"What sort of simpleton makes such a ridiculous choice?" Mr. Pelham's voice rang through the dining room. "Someone who has something to hide. I should have known that *téte-à-téte* in his drawing room wasn't an innocent conversation."

Robert opened his mouth, but she rushed the last few paces to him and squeezed his arm.

"That will not help anything," Holly whispered. Though a part of her wanted to hear him say whatever insult he'd planned for the satisfaction of seeing the shock on Mr. Pelham's face. The rest of the party could not look more horrified after Mr. Pelham's accusation.

Robert closed his mouth. And pointedly wrapped his hand over hers.

"You wanted to speak with me?" She pulled on his arm, unable to bear the stifling air of the dining room and penetrating looks from her parents any longer. His touch made it hard to breathe.

"Where are you going?" her father asked.

"He asked for a private audience." Spencer had followed Holly around the table, hands raised to soothe their father.

The color of the older man's face rivaled the juice-drenched ham on the table. "Not with my daughter."

"She's a grown woman. By law she can make this decision on her own." Her brother motioned for them to go. Holly didn't wait for her parents' protest. As fast as she dared pull him, she led Robert from the room.

The door creaked behind them, and Spencer's knowing smile peeked through the opening before it clicked shut. Holly and Robert stood alone in the hallway, lit only by a few candles.

And then she couldn't keep the bubbling emotions inside a moment longer. She threw her arms around him and pressed her cheek to his, relishing the feel of him. He buried his face against her neck, his lips brushing her skin. Like a sun waking over a gray sea, heat spread from his touch until a brilliant morning glowed within her.

"You came," she said. "I can hardly believe it."

He laughed, his arms slowly circling her waist. "I'm glad you feel that way. I've made no friends of your parents."

"My brother will sort that out." She cocked her head with a coy smile. "He owes you for his life, doesn't he?"

Robert pulled her tightly against him and rested his head on hers. "Oh, Holly, is there anything I can say to convince you to come back to Cornwall?"

She looked up into his pleading eyes.

"I know it isn't what you want," he said. "I can't be the polished, rich gentleman you deserve. But I won't make you go out in the boat again." The corners of his lips lifted. "For a time, at least."

"Very well, I will come as long as I don't have to ride in the boat."

He blinked, as though he hadn't expected acceptance.

Holly laughed and pulled on the chain around her neck, slipping the little tin heart out of its hiding place. "I did not know how much Cornwall had come to mean to me until I left it. I did not know how much you had come to mean to me."

Robert caught hold of the pendant and stroked the marred surface with his fingers. "What happened?"

"Mr. Pelham threw it in the fire." She shook her head at her own stupidity. "I should have realized then I couldn't marry that man. I nearly did something I would regret all of my life. I'm so sorry for running off, and for every unfeeling, ignorant thing I—"

Her apology was cut off by his lips against hers. Sparks that whirled within her as they spoke now burst into an ardent flame. She sighed into the warmth of his lips. How she had yearned for this since leaving him. The assertiveness of his kiss left her in no doubt that he had longed for this moment as well.

Robert's lips slowed, and he panted as he pulled away. But Holly wasn't done yet. She threaded her fingers through his sandy hair and dragged him back into the kiss. He eagerly followed. She smoothed her hands down the sides of his face.

"Can you marry a br—"

Holly clamped her hand around his mouth before he could say it. "I will marry a wonderful man, who is everything I never would have dreamed I needed to make me whole."

A tear escaped his eye, and he ducked his head. She traced it down his cheek with a trembling finger. "I love you, Robert," she whispered.

He clasped her against his chest, falling back a step from the force of his excitement. His peg leg clunked against the floor, and Holly could only beam from within his crushing embrace. She slid her arms around him under his faded navy coat, finally feeling everything was right.

Chapter Twelve

Bitter wind tore at their clothes, but Holly didn't wish to be anywhere else. Robert practically ran down the path to the sea with her in tow.

"Slow down, Robert." She couldn't sound stern if she wished. "If you fall and break your neck, I am not dragging you back to the house."

"I'll call for Spencer. He owes me for saving his skin."

"I think he already repaid that debt."

"Well, then he owes me for saving his sister."

Holly didn't argue that as they hurried faster than she'd ever seen him go. Perhaps the peg leg wasn't as bad as he thought. She had her skirts gathered in one hand to keep them out of the way. The new embroidery Aunt Margaret had helped her finish late the night before peeked out from under the hem of her old brown pelisse. None of it was new, none of it was grand, but as she stood in the church earlier that morning she had felt like a queen.

Robert slowed when he reached the sand and let go of her. After a few paces, he spread a blanket out and sat. He beckoned her over, pulling her onto his lap. His arms wound about her, as though he never intended to let go.

"What do you think, darling?"

Holly's lips screwed into a pout. "Do *not* call me that." She didn't ever want to think of the horrid man who overused the word again.

His eyes twinkled. "What shall I call you, then?"

She leaned back into him with a sigh. "Just Holly, thank you."

They watched the crashing waves and little dots of birds swirling around the distant island with its ruined lighthouse. A winter sky painted the waters a steely blue. She breathed in their lovely scent.

"I much prefer admiring the island from the shore," she said after a while.

"We can fix that sentiment," Robert said in her ear. "Broom and I salvaged the boat."

Holly shook her head.

With a tantalizing chuckle, he plucked up the heart pendant from where it rested against her coat and gently kissed it.

"I love you, Holly."

And then his lips met hers.

The End

Acknowledgments

A year ago I had no idea where my writing journey would take me. Little did I imagine I would join such an amazing group of writers. I am deeply grateful for the ladies of Love Letter Press—Sally Britton, Megan Walker, Heidi Kimball, and Joanna Barker—for their encouragement and faith in me. I'm so excited for the future of this group and for the awesome individual projects these talented writers are working on. Most importantly, I'm thankful for their friendship and love during a trying year.

I will be forever grateful to my parents for their influence. To my dad, Boyd Matheson, for showing me the importance and wonder of stories, and to my mom, Debbie Matheson, for helping me write down some of my first meager efforts.

Thanks to my amazing in-laws, Brent and Mary Carol Hawks, for their endless love and support. I could not have made it through the hard days without them. Their example of selfless service has touched my life in so many ways. I am incredibly blessed to have them in my life.

Thank you to several family members for the use of their names—my sister Sarah Matheson, my grandfather Bob Matheson, and my step-great-great-great-great-great grandfather Broom Driver.

And thanks to my brother-in-law Matthew Hawks for answering medical questions and discussing amputees' capabilities.

A shout-out to Shaela Kay for the beautiful cover, Stephanie Lance for her photography talent, and Carly Berrett for being my model.

Several beta readers helped me with typos and awkward spots, and I'm grateful for their help. Thank you Colette Campbell, Stacy Compton, Alayna Townsend, Alison Clawson, Sarah Fairbanks, and Darci McInnes. And a special shout-out to my writing buddies Deborah Hathaway and Caroline Huball for their valuable thoughts.

One of the biggest encouragements in writing is having loyal fans, and no fans have stood with me like my dear friend Bree Freeman and my amazing sisters-in-law Kathryn Hawks and Corie Hawks. My family and friends have kept me going through many trials inside and outside of writing.

Finally, none of this would have been possible without the support of my husband. Thank you for inspiring, discussing, reasoning, listening, washing dishes, putting kids to bed, and just loving this crazy, emotional writer. You are the best of the best. Love you.

About the Author

Arlem Hawks began making up stories before she could write. Living all over the Western United States and traveling around the world gave her a love of cultures and people, and the stories they have to tell. She graduated from Brigham Young University with a degree in communications and emphasis in print journalism, and now lives in Arizona with her husband and two children.

Made in the USA
Las Vegas, NV
07 March 2022

45175132R00074